Fractured Times

Short Stories from the
Ten Green Jotters

Best Wishes

Dale

Published: Amazon KDP
Cover photo: Skitterphoto via Pixabay.com

For all those who like to escape the humdrum

The Wordsmith's Poem

The Wordsmith rubbed his chin

And frowned, but sentences slept

And stayed unwound.

His mind raced back, to and fro

Until these words you see here now.

He then relaxed, unfurled his brow,

And as you read –

No more a scowl.

Peter Everard 2023

PREFACE

Welcome to the third anthology of short stories by the Ten Green Jotters!

What is Time? Is it just a way of measuring periods between events - or as Einstein said: 'An illusion'. Do memories form part of this illusion?

The 22 stories in this book are based around this theme – the present, the past, the future: nostalgia, historical events, ghosts, people transported from one time to another and even: *"What if things had happened differently?"*

Romantic, mysterious, amusing - we hope that you enjoy these eclectic and thought-provoking tales.

Ten Green Jotters 2023

CONTENTS

THE SOLUTIONS SHOP
By C.G. Harris

I hadn't noticed it before. Perhaps it's because I'm always head down, walking from my dead-end marriage to a deader-end job – or perhaps I just don't notice much of anything anymore. But there it was, no shabbier than the rest in a row of run-down Bronx shops, only with a hand-scrawled sign in the window that caught my eye: *Solutions Inside.* I stopped sharp and a guy came out chewing a match and tossing a coin. He looked at me closely from under his Derby, then chuckled familiarly. "Come on in, bud," he said.

He didn't wait but moved inside and, like a loon, I followed. I didn't like the look of him – skinny, sharp face, narrow eyes – or his manner, as though he was about to laugh out loud, but... well, who doesn't want solutions to something?

By the way, you don't know me but I'm not such a bad guy. I still love my wife, kind of. But I could have been so much more, you know what I mean? An All-State footballer shouldn't give up on talent like that. But the cocktails had kicked in over burgers at The Breslin in 2010, and she was looking damn good; the marriage love mist came down, she said "Yes" and that was it. Later it was always *'You need a job; football is for the birds'.* And she was right, sure she was. Two kids need feeding. Jeez, that night at The Breslin...I shook my head.

Inside the shop the guy turned, pulled down the blinds, locked the door and switched on a lamp in the corner. It sat on a small desk next to a screen and a keyboard; I'll admit I'm not into that stuff and when I saw there was nothing else in the room, I said to the guy that it was pretty empty for a shop that offered solutions. And what sort of solutions were they offering anyway?

"They? It's just me, bud. And a solution...to whatever you think is the problem. Here, sit down and put this on."

He pulled out from somewhere what looked like a headset with a few extra wires on top and rolled a desk chair under my ass. I put on the headset and he plugged in the lead; straightaway the screen came to life.

The guy started jabbering at me, but I held up my hand. "What do I do, and how much is it costing me?"

He looked at me kind of shrewdly and said it was straightforward enough, even for an ex-football jock like myself. I was about to ask how the hell he knew that, but he carried on.

"It's simple, see?" He leaned forward and I thought his breath would smell, but it didn't. I couldn't feel his breath at all.

"Just *think*, that's all. Look at the screen and think. About all the decisions you made in your life. If you could change one, any one at all, what would it be? When you've found it," he shrugged his shoulders, "you just press here." He pointed to a button on the keyboard that said *Alt*.

"What the hell's that mean?"

He shrugged again. "Alternative. Alter. Whatever. Oh, it don't cost you a thing. I get my kicks out of helping guys like you."

"Guys like me?"

He looked at me with those thin eyes. "Miserable, moaning, dissatisfied guys like you," he said.

"Hey! Less of the-" I started up, but he pressed the *Enter* button and I watched my life whirr and flicker before me – a lifetime of decisions squeezed into a 15-inch screen and thirty seconds. The guy stood there, chewing his match and tossing his coin.

I was getting kind of dizzy when things started slowing down and there it was in front of me. The Breslin, 2010...Janice, looking nice and pretty, eating high-end burger with just a little juice on her chin, looking at me with big, brown eyes. She was a good woman, too good for me really. But I could see several empty cocktail glasses on the table. I was about to ask her to marry me – and my football career was about to be blown.

"Stop!" I shouted.

The guy pressed a key and the image stood still. "Are you sure?" he said, quietly. "Really sure?"

I hesitated. "What's going to happen?" I whispered, just a bead or two of sweat on my lip.

The guy tossed the coin, caught it neatly and held it in a closed fist. "There's only one way to find out, bud."

I pressed *Alt* and the room went black.

*

I hadn't noticed it before. Perhaps it's because I'm always limping along head down, walking from my scummy one-bed apartment to a number of dead-end jobs – or perhaps I just don't notice much of anything anymore. But there it was, with a guy at the door in a Derby, chewing a match and tossing a coin, just another run-down shop in a whole row of them in a shabby Bronx street. Only there was a sign in the window that caught my eye: *Solutions Inside.* The guy in the hat looked at me closely and chuckled familiarly. Then he laughed out loud. "Come on in, bud," he said.

By the way, I'm not such a loser; there are people worse off...ain't there? Sure, I broke my leg making a touchdown in 2011. Ruined my football career before it took off; I was good, really I was.

I take what jobs I can get and what girlfriends will have me. That's not so bad, but I can't help it, I feel a little sorry for myself – well, a lot, and often.

If only I had married Janice; she would have been good for me alright. I should have asked her that evening at The Breslin when the cocktails kicked in over burgers. When I didn't, she left for California instead. Jeez, that night at The Breslin...

I followed the guy into his creepy little shop. I don't really like the way he looks at me as though he knows me – but who doesn't need solutions, huh? I wonder what he's offering...

GINGER NUT BILLY:
LOST AND FOUND
By Tony Ormerod

It must be close to thirty years since that bleak January afternoon in East London when I came across "The Lost Boy", as I now think of him.

An old retired friend, recently bereaved and not enjoying the best of health himself, had invited me round for a few drinks followed by a meal at his favourite local restaurant. When working with me in the city, he had frequented the place and often spoke about it with enthusiasm. I had looked forward to seeing him again ever since we agreed to meet and he gave me elaborate instructions over the telephone. These I had scribbled haphazardly onto an old envelope.

Needless to say, as was my custom, I managed to lose or mislay the envelope and I was left with the scant knowledge that my friend lived at 47 Waterloo Street and his house was quite close to an Underground station. Its name escapes me even now!

In spite of the fact that I phoned several times, without success, I was confident that the minimal information I retained in my memory would suffice.

It was close to 4 p.m. when I emerged from the station and, peering to my left and right through a fast-descending fog, I intended to ask an available pedestrian for some directions. At first glance none appeared until, a few seconds later, out of nowhere it seemed, I saw a boy walking briskly towards me.

The first thing that struck me was his hair. It was the brightest shade of red I had ever seen. As a young lad of his age, nine or ten, I had accepted with resignation the nickname Ginger, but that boy? That boy took the first prize. He came nearer and although the light was fading fast, not helped by the ever-enveloping fog, I could not fail to notice that in spite of the near freezing conditions he was coatless. Instead, he was wearing old-fashioned short grey trousers, a rather grubby off-white shirt and, peculiarly, the sort of short-sleeved multi-coloured pullover I myself was forced to wear in my early youth. Seemingly immune to the temperature, he slowed and turned to cross the road.

'Excuse me!' I halted the lad by raising a hand and he, startled, stopped in his tracks and retreated a couple of paces. 'It's alright, son,' I reassured him. 'I'm afraid I'm a little bit lost. I wonder, could you tell me where Waterloo Street is?'

The boy sniffed and drew a shirtsleeve across the underside of his nose. 'I dunno, mister,' he replied, with no apparent consideration of the question.

It was then, as he waved his hand, that I spotted something I thought I recognised clutched between his fingers. 'What have you got there in your hand?' I enquired, as kindly as I could manage.

'It's a penny, of course, mister.' He relaxed a little and held out the coin for inspection. I was right. It was an old pre-decimal penny and I could not prevent myself from laughing.

'You're not going to buy anything with that, are you?'

'Course I am! You get a lorra sweets with a penny and Aunt Lil's sweet shop is lovely.' He nodded his head and pointed a finger.

I wheeled around but all I could see was a pub about 50 yards further down on the opposite side of the road. There was no sign of any shops. I was puzzled.

'And where exactly is Aunt Lil's?' Again, he pointed his finger at the pub. 'Well, I think you are going to be disappointed, son.' I reached into my overcoat pocket and pulled out a half packet of the mints I always carried, owing to the fact that I'd just given up smoking for the third time and needed a substitute/comforter. 'Here you are, have one of these on me.'

'No thanks, mister.' There was a moment's hesitation and then he stepped off the pavement and manoeuvred his way carefully around me.

'Go on, there's no charge; you can keep your penny.'

'No. Mum says I should never take sweets from strangers.'

I shrugged, returned the mints to my pocket and privately thought that mothers were always right. Somehow, magically, the boy had disappeared. Into the pub? It seemed odd but where

5

else could he be? In any event, he was obviously ignorant of his own neighbourhood.

I waited a few seconds. The woman who I then approached and intercepted was of a good age; probably in her eighties, I surmised. Warmly dressed in a long black coat, black hat and a scarf that covered the lower half of her face, she was carrying a small bouquet clasped in front of her. It was only as I started to ask for the whereabouts of Waterloo Street that I noticed how sad and preoccupied she seemed.

'What? What did you say?'

I repeated my question, but a little more slowly.

'Oh. Sorry, yes. It's very close. Just follow this road for a couple of minutes. In fact, it's the first street you come to, on your left.'

I don't know why, but I felt compelled to regale her with my tale of the puzzling encounter with a strange boy who not only seemed unaware of his surroundings but was also under the illusion that one very old penny could buy him anything at all.

At first, she merely nodded in a polite but disinterested way, but when I mentioned the penny she became very agitated. The street lights had burst into life and I could clearly see that she was crying. The bouquet fell to the floor as she grasped one of my arms. 'Did 'e tell you 'is name?'

It seemed such a bizarre question and I could not help but smile.

'It's not funny!' She was shouting now. 'Answer me! What was 'is name?' Her grip on my arm tightened and I wondered if the poor woman was perhaps mentally ill.

'I don't know.'

I looked around in desperation and noticed another woman crossing the road and hurrying towards us. She too was warmly dressed against the cold. 'What's the matter, Carol, love?' she shouted. 'Is this bloke pestering you?' Reaching us, a little breathless, she looked ready for a fight. It seemed ludicrous. I was offended and embarrassed for myself when a few more people who had emerged from the bowels of the Underground gathered close by.

Carol ignored everyone. 'What's the colour of 'is 'air?' she demanded, shaking my arm. 'Tell me, is 'e a ginger nut?'

6

'Why yes; in fact, he has the brightest red hair I've ever seen.'

I can only describe her reaction to this information as shocking. She fell to her knees and I will never forget the sound of her unnatural, shrieking voice. 'Oh, me poor lost boy, me poor Billy.'

She repeated herself and then, alarmingly, clutching at her chest, she collapsed and fell full length onto the pavement. Her friend, her best friend Barbara as I discovered a little later, urged someone, anyone to quickly run to the telephone box situated outside the station entrance to summon an ambulance. More immediate help was provided when a young, smartly dressed young man called out that he was already contacting the emergency services using his mobile phone.

Announcing herself as a nurse, another onlooker stepped forward and, kneeling down beside the ominously still body, did all she could to revive poor Carol. Finally, after a couple of minutes, it was obvious that her efforts had been in vain.

I was in a state of shock myself and felt guilty, wondering if, unwittingly, I had somehow caused a death. Naturally, I waited until the ambulance had arrived and departed and it was then, after the small gathering had slowly dispersed, that I was given an explanation by a weeping Barbara.

I somehow held myself together, wracked with guilt, until I gathered from her that the poor dead woman had suffered serious heart problems. The two friends had known each other since their primary school days. Young Billy, aged nine – Carol's only son – had been killed when one of the last V2 rockets targeting London fell out of the sky and onto a sweet shop in 1945. The shopkeeper – his Aunt Lilian, his mother's sister – had also perished.

I shook my head in disbelief. I had always been a sceptic, a man who distrusted dubious tales of ghosts and things that went bump in the night – but that episode? That was real.

'When did the rocket hit?' I enquired of Barbara. She stopped crying and thought for a moment.

'Well, would you believe it, January the fifth. That's today, isn't it?'

'It is indeed, and it's fifty years ago!'

I glanced down and noticed what was left of the pathetic little bouquet, which had been forgotten. I should have done something myself but, rather ungallantly, unthinkingly, I watched as an unsteady Barbara stooped and picked it up. Dabbing her eyes with a handkerchief, she turned to me. 'I'd better put these where Carol would 'ave wanted them.'

'Where's that?' I enquired.

'There,' she pointed, 'outside the pub. It's where Lil's sweetshop used to be.'

I did not see the need to say anything else except to lamely wish her luck for the future and then, slowly, she disappeared into the fog, leaving me with my own thoughts.

I was still blaming myself for accidentally causing the death of an old lady, but Barbara had said, through her tears, that: 'It could 'ave 'appened at any time. Don't worry, sir.' But I could not help worrying about it, together with the unsettling, strange and frankly frightening encounter with what was surely the ghost of a long dead, still loved young boy.

All alone now, after standing for a full minute close to the spot where Carol had so tragically died, I crossed the road to resume my search for Waterloo Street. There was no traffic, no pedestrians and all I could hear were my own footsteps as I approached the pub, which was, unsurprisingly, only just visible. Somehow, it suddenly turned much colder.

'Ello again, mister!'

There could be no mistaking the voice, but what emerged from the murk to within a few yards of me was not the same Billy. To my horror there was no face, just a bloody mess beneath a mop of bright red hair. One whole arm reached out to me. In the hand were the remains of a small paper bag. 'I told yer me Aunt Lil sold nice sweets; do yer want one?'

The lad staggered towards me. At that moment, as I swiftly backed away in preparation to flee, disgusted, horrified, and terrified in equal measure, what I can only describe as "a shape" hovered and moved towards the two of us.

'Billy, you little devil!' it shouted. 'What 'ave I told you about talking to strangers?'

I was never an athlete and, although I was not at that time a young man, I swear I have never run as fast as I did that winter afternoon all those years ago.

CHECKMATE
By Glynne Covell

The beautiful, majestic elephant was down. Still struggling pathetically as the poachers encircled the mighty beast, his strength was waning as, with tendons deliberately cut, his tusk brutally slashed, he was slowly becoming weaker, bleeding to death, succumbing to his fate.

Ali, the leader, administered the final blow, plunging the rusty javelin-like iron into the poor animal's chest. A heart-breaking screech emanated from the creature, a final hopeless tossing of the flaccid trunk and then silence. A great cheer went up from the poachers, who revelled in the death of another victim before they set about removing the enormous tusks with their saws. Two young bewildered calves who had watched their father's slaughter ran into the scrub, terrified, screaming and helpless. They did not have tusks so were not worthy of attention.

It was 1941 and the poachers would argue that it was a case of survival for them and their families that justified the evil, callous treatment of these creatures. Many would disagree and struggled with the knowledge of what was happening in the forest. Ali's son was one such boy. It upset him beyond words as he worked with his father's men to load the tusks onto the back of the truck. He felt the pain, the utter cruelty and cried helplessly as he watched the young elephants run away from the destruction. Who is to say which creature on earth should die?

'Stop your sobbing like a girl, Malik!' shouted Ali as he forcefully hit the boy around the head. 'You want to eat, don't you, and look after your mother and the little ones?' Malik fell to the ground with the blow.

Malik got up, nodded and wiped his eyes on his grubby, torn shirt, smeared with elephant's blood. He knew he could never accept such brutal murder of these beautiful animals, but Baba was right; life was all about survival here in Ceylon. Once the tusks were cut down and removed, he would go with Baba to market to sell the precious loot and then the rupees would be divided out between the poachers. It was big money.

It was a long day and young Malik was exhausted, physically and emotionally. Finally, the precious loot was secured on the trucks and the small convoy was ready to move out. All that was left was the massacred mess of a once proud beast, butchered for his teeth, his life on earth brought to a bloody end for man.

Malik travelled with his father the following day, taking the tusks to a nearby village where a man, Abha, and his sons bought one load and dragged it back to their home. Malik followed on as he knew two of the young lads and often went to watch them work with their father. They scrubbed, cleaned and polished the ivory and then finally chiselled them into exquisite figurines. Knights and bishops, castles, kings and queens and pawns. Remarkable workmanship: a skill handed down from Abha's great grandfather. No thought was given to the fine animal who had been sacrificed to enable this family to make a few rupees. Their focus was on the perfect pieces carved from this beautiful material. Malik stood watching, in awe of the skill used, but at the same time his eyes filled with tears again for the elephants who suffered.

His young friends, Manvik and Yuvaan enjoyed helping their father and learning the art of this craft. Yuvaan showed Malik exactly how he worked; Malik sat patiently, absorbed in the talent as the coveted material took shape as a chess piece. They had explained before about this logical game and he was mesmerized, both by the techniques used to create such masterpieces of fine work and for this highly skilled, strategic game. How he would rather do such work instead of witnessing the barbaric killing involved.

Yuvaan always chiselled his initials underneath the queen, a Y and C, Yuvan Chopra. 'You see, Malik, my friend, I am famous!' he said. They laughed.

Days later, the completed figures were taken to the port of Trincomalee, where they were sold to tourists and seamen who, knowing ivory to be priceless and desirable, gave not one thought to their origin or manufacture.

Malik's story did not end there. One of the sets that evolved from this ivory made its way to England in the trunk of able seaman Elmer Covell at the end of the war. His family were thrilled to see such perfection in the sculpting of these valuable chess pieces and for some years it stood proudly on the mantelpiece in Elmer's home, dusted regularly by his mother, Harriet. She often picked them up, stroked the smooth material, marvelled at the unblemished work and was always proud to show them off to visitors and neighbours, saying they had come all the way from Ceylon. How incredible that God made such perfection. Unfortunately, no one could play the game and they remained unused, standing remains of the elephant which no one gave a thought to.

Sadly, a few years later, Elmer's sister, Barbara died tragically in childbirth, leaving her husband and her only son, Tom. Tom was an exceptionally gifted child and when Elmer kindly gave him the chess set, he quickly learned the technique of the game and treasured the heirloom.

Many years passed and when Tom, a prominent and qualified chemist, left England with his wife and went to live in Canada, he took the chess set with him. He often thought of Uncle Elmer, who had entrusted it to him. The family, which had originated in Rotherhithe, split up and Tom lost all contact.

Until, into the following century, Tom's daughter, Helen, living in Alberta, Canada, researched the family tree. That led to her contacting some of seaman Elmer Covell's descendants back in England and, thanks to her, Tom developed a close relationship with a young lad, Zeyd. The boy, 70 years younger than himself, was a cousin twice removed. Nearing the end of his life, Tom, wishing the chess set to remain in the family, sent the heirloom to him. The pieces of ivory tusk had travelled halfway around the world and now moved on again to England.

Zeyd, that distant cousin, fingered the exquisite priceless ivory, thoughts of beautiful, sacrificed elephants torturing his mind. He looked at the carved letters of Y and C, pondering on the life of the person who had no doubt handled these figures. He was playing with a friend, Samuel.

'Life's so unfair, Sam,' he said. 'What a hard life some people have. Some poor souls are born to an endless struggle of survival. Just awful to think that these pieces were part of an elephant's tusks but probably it was a matter of life and death for the poachers. We're not in that position. How can we judge?'

Sam was deep in thought over his next move, pondering whether to sacrifice his bishop. 'You're right, Zeyd. We're so damned lucky here where we have choice. Some just don't.'

As Zeyd slowly removed the bishop from the board, he eyed the workmanship of the figure again. This chess set had inspired his logical, mathematical mind and he was now extremely adept at the game, winning tournaments at school. It was in that moment, whilst he reflected on the inhumane practices in the world, that he determined his future would be in conservation. Cruelty in the world, sadly, would never end. But every little step would help. If he could save just one creature from being unnecessarily slaughtered, his input would be worth it.

Maybe if Malik had known that, in the distant future, the very ivory he had been involved in would inspire a lad of his age to help protect and stand up for the lives of such animals, he would perhaps have had some comfort.

'Aha, Sam, thank you for your bishop. But now, my friend… Checkmate!'

Sam laughed and threw up his hands in defeat. He had not seen that coming. Zeyd's skill at the game was a force to be reckoned with. He surrendered his queen and he too contemplated the initials YC underneath the ivory figure.

Hopefully, Zeyd thought, it is not too late for man to change the fortune of some species. We must checkmate extinction.

*

Note:
Scientists have found that evolution is apparently at work already whereby elephants born without tusks are becoming more common. Not all elephant breeds grow tusks and as the horrific practice of murdering them for their horns has depleted their numbers, those without such magnificent features are becoming the more evident and common species.

JULIE'S JOURNEY
By Jan Brown

As they entered the tunnel, Julie tensed. The familiar clackety clack of wheels on track intensified and built to a shriek. She looked around at the other passengers, who were engrossed in their newspapers, unconcerned by such fantasies as shrieking trains. Julie clasped her great-grandfather's fob watch as the train raced on.

*

"Julie love, do you want tea?"

"No, Mum. How many times do I have to tell you, I hate tea."

"Oh yes, sorry love, I forget. You used to love a milky tea when you were a little 'un."

"But I'm a 31-year-old divorcee now, living back with her parents, and I'm really upset about all that, so please don't force bloody milky tea on me as well!" Julie glared over at her crestfallen mother. "Sorry, Mum, I'm a bit stressed. I'll have a strong coffee. That'd be lovely."

"OK, love, don't worry. Where's Bowie?"

"He's curled up on my bed at the moment, fast asleep. He's explored the local area, checked out the competition and overdosed on catnip."

"Bless him, he seems to have settled in well."

Julie nodded. "Yes, love him. I'm so relieved that Matt let me keep him. If I'd lost Bowie as well, that would have finished me off."

"Oh, love." Molly hugged her daughter. "You're stronger than that. You'll bounce back, you know. We make our women strong in Penge."

"Hmm, thanks Mum. Anyway, where's Dad this evening?"

"He's on the late shift at the library, eight o'clock finish and probably nine before he actually gets out and locks up." Molly patted Julie on the shoulder as she headed towards the kitchen.

"Speaking of which, I'd better get him a sandwich ready. He won't want a heavy meal late at night."

"OK. I'm off to bed, Mum. I'll take my coffee with me."

"Hmm, I'm not sure that's a good idea. You know that stuff's hardly going to help you drop off."

Julie headed upstairs, the warning about coffee keeping you awake at night echoing in her ears. By 3 am, she had to admit her mum was probably right. She had listened to music on her radio, but every song somehow reminded her of Matt: of something lovely he had said or done, a special holiday they had enjoyed together, or a sudden inexplicable argument or accusation. Julie ripped out the earphones and threw them across the floor. She picked up a book, but every other word drew her mind to Matt; either the hero or the villain was tall, dark and handsome, and also irritating, opinionated and overbearing.

Julie sighed and tossed the book in the general direction of the earphones. "What am I going to do with myself, Bowie?" The cat surveyed her with his huge eyes, one golden and one green, before turning attention to washing himself.

She hadn't expected to sleep, but was awakened next morning by the joyful sound of sparrows twittering in the cherry tree in the front garden. Julie lay in bed watching Bowie through sleepy eyes as he prowled up and down on the window sill, making his little chuttering sounds at the birds. Finally, the early morning harmony was disrupted by the not so lovely roar of Simon from next-door-but-one's motorbike racing off towards the station.

"Honestly, Mum, isn't he a bit old for all that hot metal stuff?" Julie slumped over the kitchen table, swirling a teaspoon in her coffee.

"He fancies himself 'cos no one else will!" Molly retorted.

"Mum!" Julie laughed. "That's a bit rude for you."

"Just good to see you smile, love. Will you take your dad up a cup of tea? He did have a late one last night, so I thought he deserved a bit of a lie in. Not too much though, don't want him getting used to luxury!"

"Course. Give it here."

*

"Morning, Dad. Mums sent you up a cup of tea, but she said to tell you you're not allowed to sleep in!" Julie smiled down at her dad and perched on the edge of the bed, cradling the mug.

"Morning, Julie love. Yes, I bet she did." Tony shuffled up the bed and, reaching over to the bedside table, groped for his glasses. "Here, give us that tea." He took a huge gulp and sighed. "Perfect. You can't beat the first cuppa." He paused. "Now then, young lady, how are you?"

"Dad, you're giving me one of your serious looks. What's going on?"

"It's just me and your mum, we're both worried about you. We don't like to see you so unhappy."

"Oh, so it wasn't just about bringing you up a cup of tea then? Honestly, I'm OK. Glad to be back with my family."

"But?" Tony stuck out his lower lip and nodded at her encouragingly, the remaining tufts of dark hair bobbing crazily on his head.

"Dad, you're making me laugh pulling that face!"

"Talk to me, Han. Serious now."

Julie shifted and shuffled her feet. "I think I'm just a bit lost. I don't know what to do with myself – and I know what you're going to say." Julie held her hands up as if she knew her dad's thoughts. "I had a perfectly good job and threw it away... but I couldn't stay working in the same office as Matt. It was killing me." She blinked the tears away rapidly until she could see her father again.

"Oh Han, of course you couldn't stay there. We're definitely in the sexist seventies. It's really bad that it's nearly always the woman who has to leave if an office romance goes wrong." He screwed up his face with annoyance.

"Wow, go Dad." Julie smiled sheepishly. 'Thank you. I really appreciate your support, and Mum's. Anyway, you'd better drink that tea and get up or there'll be a home romance going wrong!"

"Ha, yes I don't want to upset your mum! But hang on a minute, I have something for you." Tony leaned over to open his bedside cabinet and pulled out a silver fob watch carefully nestled in tissue paper. "This used to belong to my father, and his father before him. It's very special to me."

"Oh Dad, it's lovely. But what am I going to do with it?"

"Your great granddad, Bert was involved in the construction of Penge railway tunnel, all one mile and 381 yards of it. Sorry if I'm being a bit of a bore, love, but I'm so proud of him. He worked hard for this watch, and that tunnel is the longest constructed in the south east. I know how you used to love history at school. I thought you might like to do a bit of family research?" Julie turned the watch in its tissue paper, the Roman numerals sparkling in the morning light. Tony watched her carefully. "If you're not interested, it's fine."

"No, Dad, you're right. It'll give me something useful to do and at the very least the next time I travel through the tunnel I can think about my great grandfather having a hand in building it. Thanks, Dad." She stepped from the bedroom almost lightly.

Tony smiled and clenched his fist. "Result."

*

That Sunday morning was bright and sunny. The dew sparkling on the grass somehow put a little spring in Julie's step and she found herself fairly marching to the station, her boots clicking rhythmically on the pavement, her purple doubled-breasted blazer buttoned up against the early morning chill. She had only decided the previous night to make the journey to London through the tunnel.

"Why tomorrow of all days, Julie?" her mother had asked. "I thought we could go to the Bromley Mansion for Sunday lunch."

"No, you and Dad have had to babysit me too much lately. I need to do something for myself – and you two can have a lovely lunch together."

"Where are you going to go?" Her father had looked concerned. "There's not much to do in London on a Sunday morning, you know."

"I don't know, Dad. Maybe walk through the parks."

Julie smiled to herself as she recalled the look on his face as he'd said, "You've got Crystal Palace Park up the road for that, all 200 acres of it, monkeys and all. Hey, you're not meeting that Matt again, are you? He's no good for you, that one."

Julie had bristled. "I'm not a fool, Dad. He's well gone. I just want to do something different; I suppose. Have a bit of an adventure."

*

Julie watched as the green six-carriage train trundled begrudgingly into Penge East station and huffled to a halt. Just one man alighted, dressed in a colourful outfit of blue corduroy trousers and darker blue turtleneck sweater. His chunky heels echoed down the platform until he disappeared out into Station Square.

Having easily found an empty carriage, Julie settled back and waited for the 10.25 am to begin its journey to Victoria. Finally, the stationmaster shouted: "Stand away, stand away!" After a moment's hesitation, the train kicked itself into life and began an unwilling, languid chug towards the dark mouth of Penge tunnel and slowly into the tunnel itself. Immediately, daylight was extinguished, replaced by a weak orange glow from the carriage lights. Julie tapped her feet against the wooden boards in annoyance as the train showed no sign of speeding up.

"Must you do that, young lady?"

Julie jerked upright. She must have fallen asleep as she'd not noticed anyone entering the carriage from the corridor. "Oh. sorry." She smiled hopefully at the rather severe-looking older lady, dark hair pulled back in a bun, but received just a suspicious glare.

The carriage door was abruptly pulled back and two men rushed in from the corridor, breathing noisily. "Michael, we only just made it! We can't be that late again."

Michael, clad in wide-collared pink shirt and diamond pullover, chuckled. "Come on, Toad, we're on holiday. Just relax!" Toad merely huffed himself into a corner seat. The four travelling companions continued their ponderous journey in traditional British Rail silence with even the two friends not saying much.

"Do you know if it's always this slow?' Julie asked, shuddering as she remembered her father's pride at the length of the tunnel. "At this rate we'll never get to the other end, and the lighting is terrible in here."

"Patience," a solitary voice, probably Miss Prim, commented in the gloom.

The train slowed even further to a miniscule crawl, seemingly waiting for the signal to spring forward, before jolting into action. Now rapidly building up speed, the clackety clack of the wheels intensified into a shriek and the lights flickered erratically off and on. As the train hurtled on, the carriage rocking violently from side to side, accompanied by a prolonged howl from the tunnel walls, Julie reached into her pocket and clasped the fob watch tightly, thinking of the great great grandfather she had never known.

A sudden, vicious, thunderous crack outside the carriage and the squealing of brakes was followed by absolute darkness and stillness within it.

"Err, hello?" Julie whispered into the terrifying silence through numb dry lips, her heart pumping painfully, as if ready to leap from her body.

"Are you alright, miss?"

"Thank goodness!" Julie had never felt so relieved to hear another voice. It sounded like one of the two companions; certainly not the stiff unfriendliness of Miss Prim. "I'm fine, thank you, but is anyone hurt?" she asked. "That was scary – and it's so dark in here."

"Don't fret, miss. The lights will come back on. They just need to light them again."

"What you fretting about, ducks?" Another voice in the dark, a different voice. Julie shuddered. Ducks?! Who was that?

The train somehow shook itself back to life and lurched forward, Julie hoped towards the end of the tunnel. She peered through the window but could only make out mysterious shapes that were just a bit darker and firmer than the surrounding darkness. Finally, the train emerged from the tunnel into glorious sunlight. Julie heaved a massive sigh of relief; next stop, Sydenham Hill. Hoping for some relieved eye contact, Julie glanced around at her fellow passengers but could only stare in wide-eyed shock. They all appeared to have changed their clothes. Miss Prim was wearing some sort of heavy black velvet gown and what could only be described as a bonnet. The two friends had on dark thigh-length coats, high stiff colours and both carried tall hats.

There was another passenger whom Julie had somehow not even noticed. The old woman was painfully thin and wearing just a dark woollen coat and grubby bonnet. She grinned toothlessly at Julie and nodded her dirty head. "Hello, ducks."

"What's going on? Is this some sort of joke?" Julie looked around desperately, noticing with a sick feeling that no one was smiling.

"Are you indisposed, miss?" asked the person named Toad.

"Watch yourself, Thomas," his companion whispered, muttering something about fallen women.

"You're all dressed differently!" Julie shouted out, suddenly aware of the glances she was getting. Looking down, she was comforted to see she was still wearing her own clothes.

"Really, young lady, you have no right to judge any respectable person. You are wearing an appalling costume; I wouldn't even allow my under-stairs servant to dress so shamefully." Miss Prim stared down her extensive, rather hairy nose. "You will never find a husband in 1870 looking like that."

"S…sorry, what did you say?" Julie slumped back onto the plush green seat as her legs gave out, unable to take in the horror of what she was hearing.

Miss Prim nodded and allowed herself a satisfied smirk. "I suspected as much. Simple, are you, or taken with the drink? Do you even know your name?"

Julie felt somehow pinned to the carriage seat and she wilted under the relentless gaze of her fellow passengers as the journey continued. Finally summoning her inner strength, she rushed to change carriages at West Dulwich and spent the remainder of her journey to London in an empty carriage, relieved that no one could see the tears trickling down her blotchy, puffy face.

With no idea what to do, Julie stared out of the window, oblivious to the changing environment flashing past as London town drew nearer. *At least I'll be less noticeable in London,* she told herself, hugging her jacket around her. Her new deep pink Laura Ashley peasant dress and long frilly blouse coat had been a 'make you feel better' present from her parents, and her button-down boots a thrilling find in a junk shop.

*

Victorian London was as noisy, smelly and dirty as Julie remembered from her history lessons, but it was also full of life. There were no cars but plenty of horse-drawn carriages and carts, and relentless shouting from street sellers. Thin, mucky-faced children dodged around smart city gentlemen and, occasionally, pairs of well-dressed ladies who ventured daringly into one of the new tearooms, their plush velvet gowns swishing and sweeping the dirty ground. Julie's shoulders drooped as she noticed with dismay that her Laura Ashley dress left her calves and ankles boldly displayed for all Victorian London to view.

"'Ere, miss, are you lost then? You don't look like a cadger." A small child, clad in rags, stared up at her, daring even to reach out and pull at the thin fabric of her dress. "I can help you for a ha'penny."

Julie thought quickly, then bent down to the child's level. "Yes. I am lost. If you can help me, you can have my lovely jacket to sell."

"Why?" He stared at her, unblinkingly.

"I've been invited to a party and I can't go like this."

"No." He nodded slowly in agreement.

"So, do you know who could make my dress look more like the other ladies' dresses?"

"Follow me!" The child darted off down a side alley, then stopped. Seeing that Julie hadn't even moved, he waved wildly at her. "Come on."

"Alright, slow down." Julie found it difficult to match his pace. Even in London the streets were full of holes and huge puddles to dodge. Finally, as he ran into another shabby, deserted alleyway, Julie came to a halt. Was this a trap?

"Come on, miss." He urged her towards a battered doorway. "My grandmother can help."

Julie looked in all directions and then followed warily. The door opened onto five crumbling steps leading into a basement area.

"Look." He pointed through a hole in the wall. Julie squinted in at an elderly lady sitting at a battered old table, patiently stitching her way through swathes of dark green fabric.

"Well now, Albert, who do we have here?"

"She's not a cadger or a thief. She wants our help." He rushed on, enthusiastically. "She needs a dress to go to a party, 'cos she can't wear that." Albert stuck his puny little chest out with pride and gestured dismissively at Julie's outfit, failing to notice her furiously blinking away the tears. Julie stood awkwardly in the doorway, aware she was being assessed by the old woman.

"Come in, my dear."

Julie moved into the small room, trying not to stare around at the obvious poverty. "What's your name?" she asked, finally. "I can't just call you Albert's grandmother."

"I am known as Myrtle McCartney, dressmaker – and you are?"

"Julie Moffett – and you don't know how happy I am to hear you're a dressmaker. I really need a decent dress."

"Do you have money?"

"I don't have the right coins with me, but I will give you a wonderful pink jacket. It's a beautiful colour and I love it so much, and…" Julie came to a halt.

"You sound desperate, my dear. Are you in trouble?"

Myrtle, head cocked to one side, reminded Julie of a tiny lively sparrow. To her horror, Julie's eyes filled with tears, thankfully unshed, at this unexpected kind concern. "Well, sort of. I mean, I'm not a bad person but I've managed to find myself here and it's not home and I don't know how I'm going to get back."

Myrtle nodded with understanding. "I too am a long way from my homeland, so I will help you. I fear I will fail to make you a new dress, but let us see what can be made from my scraps. I will take your topcoat; it may be that your strange fabric will help Albert and me regain some past comfort." She broke off abruptly to warn Julie: "It is well to remember never to allow a man to gain control over your body or possessions, for you will likely regret your actions."

A little over an hour later, Julie stepped cautiously up the steps and into the relative daylight of the alleyway, her feet cosily encased in her familiar button-down boots. Julie's pink Laura Ashley dress now had a generous dark green border that hid her calves and brushed the dirty pavements. She felt uncomfortable in the full-length gown but was thankful for the anonymity it offered – and at least her boots were familiar to walk in.

"Thank you so much." Impulsively, Julie turned and hugged the tiny woman, who beamed at her.

"Oh now, I hope you find your way home. Albert, will you come and bid your friend goodbye?"

Albert, who had long since lost interest in the proceedings, left behind his pile of stones of varying colours and sizes and took her hand. "Bye, Miss Julie. I hope you get home."

"Thank you, Albert. Thank you so much for your help and for introducing me to your grandmother. Myrtle, I hope the jacket helps you in some way, but do take care and get away from here soon."

"Well, miss, we do have some plans to move away from London, into one of the parishes, maybe Kent or Surrey. My poor boy Albert has weak lungs, and I am hopeful the country air will help him."

"That will be exciting for you both. A new life." Julie smiled at them, but sounded distracted. Her mind was buzzing. *Albert – Bert. Could it be possible?* "I must try to get home now," she added, "but take this." She pulled out a shiny 1970 silver sixpence she had discovered in her blouse pocket and passed it to Albert.

"What is it?" he asked, puzzled.

"It's money from the future. One day when you're old you'll recognise it, and maybe even remember me."

"Another invention?"

"Yes, but I didn't invent it – I just had it in my pocket. But now it's yours."

Waving, Julie stepped out into the main bustling street still looking back at her new friends. Now to get back to Penge, but which Penge did she want to get back to and who would she meet?

*

23

"Oh, I say, watch out there." Julie finding herself grabbed firmly by the arms looked up in shock at a tall handsome man, and stared into the deepest bluest eyes she'd ever seen.

"You do know you nearly went under the wheels of that horse and carriage? You should watch where you're going."

"Nonsense, he was nowhere near me." Julie took a step back "And you shouldn't go round grabbing unsuspecting females."

"My dear girl, I regard myself as a gentleman - and as a gentleman it's my duty to save the fairer sex."

He bowed low and as he came up took Julie's right hand and briefly pressed it to his lips which Julie couldn't help noticing were soft and generous.

"Well," he drawled, sweeping his hand through his dark, restless curls "this is a puzzle indeed. Do I risk asking the beautiful lady to take tea with me or should we make our goodbyes?"

"I suppose a cup of tea would be appreciated - I am probably a little in shock - but I should know your name. I don't drink tea with strangers."

"My name is Lord Matthias Garwood." Again, he bowed magnificently, and the beautiful lady is …?"

Julie snorted in a very unladylike manner. "Not about to get involved with another Garwood, thank you very much! And it's rude to stand there with your mouth open, the flies will get in."

Clutching the pocket watch tightly, for she instinctively felt this was her means of escape, Julie took a last look at the hustle and bustle of Victorian London and began walking swiftly in the direction of the railway station.

"I'm a 1970s woman and its time I went home."

RED ALERT
By A.J.R Kinchington

The hairs on the back of Alison's neck prickled. There it was, that unearthly wail; short panicky gasps of pain.

It was the herald of tragedy.

*

Although it was only four in the afternoon it was dark outside and, curtains drawn, coal fire burning brightly, the cottage was cosy.

Alison loved her home. The cottage was in a row of six on the estate of Kinlochheath Lodge. The views across farmland and the ancient pine forest had helped soothe the ache she felt after her husband Sandy died six years ago. Their daughter Kirsty had helped her relocate from Aviemore to Dalwhinnie which was seven miles to Carrbridge heading south towards Perth.

The storm was picking up its skirts and readying itself for another spectacular show, which made Alison's sense of foreboding grow. After making tea, she switched on her TV. The weather forecast at five o'clock warned of the forthcoming storm and winds of seventy miles an hour. She paced the floor, all the while checking the traffic on her mobile phone, which told of road closures due to earlier flooding and yellow weather warnings.

The wind whistled down the chimney and the rain began thudding on the windows, anxious to be let in away from the wind. Alison pulled on her sweater, sat with her book and tried to quell her fears by rationalizing that storms do blow over. Winter in the Scottish Highlands was not for the faint-hearted. Still, that wailing made her shiver; she knew what it meant.

Her mobile pinged with a message from Kirsty. She was held up at Glasgow airport, her flight cancelled because of the storm. If weather permitted, she would be home tomorrow. Alison felt disappointed, but grateful the airline was taking precautions.

Kirsty, in her second year at art school, was due home for the start of the Christmas holidays.

As the time moved around to nine thirty, the storm grew louder. Above it, the howling became more insistent. Under her breath, Alison whispered, "Please God."

The banging on her door startled her but, on opening it, she was relieved to see a familiar face. "Come in, come in! Jamie, what are you doing out in this weather?"

"Hi, Mrs. Angus. On my way to see my Gran Fraser. Needed to stop by."

"Get out of your wet coat and I'll make us some tea. How's your gran?"

"Well, she had a wee fall, but mostly bruised pride." Jamie smiled. Alison thought it reminiscent of the young boy who had been friends with Kirsty at school.

"So, how long are you home for? Maybe you and Kirsty can catch up now you're both home from your studies."

"I don't know." He paused. "I can't say. I'll have to see how I am."

While Jamie sat at the fireside Alison busied herself in the kitchen, distracted and anxious about the sounds of the night. "Jamie, stay with me," she said. "I don't want you to go."

He looked up at her, a faraway look in his eyes. "I wonder if the edge of the world feels like this; the daunting uncertainty of what is to come."

Something in his manner, his voice, made Alison's heart constrict. She did not, could not reply. Emotionally tired, she sat down, unsteadily. They sat in companionable silence.

In a while, Jamie rose and pulled on his coat. "It's all over, Mrs. Angus. I'm away to see my mother. Look in on Gran for me. Thank you for staying with me."

Alison felt a shiver down her back and was close to tears as she embraced him warmly. "Take care, Jamie. Safe journey on."

She sat and dozed and awoke to silence. No sounds of the storm, no howling. It was ten o'clock and the night was eerily silent. Unnerved by the night's events, Alison went wearily to bed.

*

Next morning, Kirsty arrived, tired and tearful. "Mum, it has been an awful night. Delays and accidents. Did you get caught in the storm?"

"No, thankfully. The storm was fierce here too. Jamie called in just after nine."

"What?" Kirsty was wide eyed. "Mum, you haven't heard. Sit down. Last night Jamie had an accident. One of the big distillery lorries was turning out onto the road and crashed into his car. The paramedics tried to keep him alive for over a half-hour, but he died at the scene."

Alison sat motionless. "What time was that?"

"It was around nine thirty."

Alison felt the world shift on its axis and reveal to her all that is certain and uncertain in time.

They looked at each other; the disbelief on Kirsty's face was met with a sure, steady gaze from Alison. "I heard the dog," she said. "He warned – as he always does."

"Mum, I know the story of the Red Dog of Badenoch. It's just folklore."

"No, Kirsty. No one has seen it except those who have had a near-death experience. They describe the dog as large, red, and it runs along the roadside yelping and howling. It knows death is imminent."

"But Jamie..." Kirsty trailed off.

"I know what I heard, and Jamie was here. He needed a safe place before his journey. He was suspended between the unseen world of life eternal and life on earth. He said he was going to see his mother. I thought it was a strange thing to say; his mother died two years ago. He asked me to look in on his gran. He was as real to me as you are now. I didn't connect Jamie to the howling earlier in the day. There have been so many accidents on the road at the foot of the glen."

Kirsty took her mother's hand and led her to the chair by the hearth. The red embers of last night's fire glowed and had both Alison and Kirsty drawing near to it; perhaps it had drawn Jamie in, in much the same way.

"Mum, you have told me about the gift of premonition that you inherited from granny. Is that what happened yesterday?"

"Well, sometimes it does not feel like a welcome gift, but if I was here to hold Jamie in the moments before his death, then maybe it is meant for me."

*

In the days that followed, both women knew the numbness of grief.

The local TV station reported on the storm damage and the accident that led to the death of a young man. The emergency team had worked hard to keep him alive; despite his injuries, he had died peacefully. It was obvious that even experienced medics felt the heavy emotions of frustration and loss. There had been a further five accidents on the busy A9 that night and local campaigners were in talks with road planners to alter speed limits and keep drivers safe.

Alison listened to the broadcast with a heavy heart. No doubt she would hear of further accidents – and the warning that chilled her to the bone.

Alison always kept her fire lit, even in summer.

TESTING TIMES
By Richard Miller

Hello, my name is Larry.

I remember this time once when I wandered into the big room, and it was full of humans. They were so much taller and bigger than me and were gathered around a table, drinking and eating. I find it strange that they stand on two legs rather than four; I can position myself on two but after a while it hurts.

The food and drink didn't look very nice. What's wrong with the stuff I eat? I hoped one of them would see me and give me my own food. I did feel hungry but then I always feel that way. Don't humans realise we cats are always on the lookout for food? Maybe I'd have to go elsewhere to eat.

I'd learned to understand the strange-looking humans a little even when they sometimes shouted at me – especially if I lay on a chair – but this time was different. Their voices were strange and a few of them weren't walking properly. The last time I had seen such behaviour was in the days when they didn't cover their mouths. How could they breathe with their mouths covered? Very odd.

I looked at the top of the table again. On it was a round object and poking out of it were sticks with fires on them. Do people eat sticks with fires? At that moment, one of the humans in the room bent down and tickled me behind the ears. How is it that they know I like that? Another then tickled me under the chin. With that, I started purring. I tried it on a bit a few moments later; I started to meow, as I knew that was a sure-fire way of getting fed.

While I was doing that, another human walked into the room. Now, I have fur all over my body and I like to keep it clean and tidy. This one's fur on his head looked messy and stuck up all over the place. Even the others in the room kept themselves neat. This was the scruffy one, who often took an animal I call my enemy for a walk. That creature always had something around its neck that someone held onto to make sure it didn't run off. I don't need anything around my neck; independent, that's me. That animal's got to be my inferior, surely?

I often wonder why the humans only have fur on their heads. How do they keep warm? Perhaps it's the strange things they wear. Over the years, I've also noticed they get up close to objects that are hot. I don't – those things hurt.

The one with the unruly fur on its head was surrounded by the others and they started hitting him on the back, but he didn't seem to mind. I found that strange, as I don't like being touched like that and have scratched and bitten those who have hurt me. I've had to do that a lot to the one being struck.

One of the others went to the table and picked up the round thing with sticks and fires. She and all the others except the one with the messy fur started making a strange noise together. The scruffy one then blew on the round thing and the fires went out. That scared me a bit. Everyone else picked up things they drank out of, raised them in the air and shouted out. The things they drank from looked very different to those I drink from. Sometimes I don't understand these humans. Why can't they be normal?

The scruffy one had lived in the building for a while, and I'd got used to him even though I didn't always like him. When he first came to the place, someone else I had grown to like disappeared. I often wondered where she went. I had noticed that the untidy one usually covered his legs – unless he rolled around with the one who picked up the round thing, when the two of them made strange noises. The person who disappeared sometimes covered her legs and other times not.

I liked the first human who had disappeared, and I think she liked me. She often stroked and tickled me and would even give me treats of food and drink. The messy one didn't like me as much; probably because I had fights with the animal known as my enemy, and I usually won those. He has the scars to prove that. Even the cat who lived nearby was nicer, and we've had a couple of fights; I always won those, mind.

Many days and nights after that time with the fires on sticks being blown out, the scruffy one left the building for good and another, who looked a lot smarter, came in. I recognised her smell from before. We cats rely on smell so much. I'm sure we can smell things that humans can't. That must make us superior. Like the one before the messy one, she was friendly to me and I hoped she would stay for a long time.

However, just as I was getting used to her, she left. What is about some humans? Can't they stay in one place for long? We cats feel happy when we stay in the same place.

I remember once being taken in a big metal box that roared and moved on four round things to a somewhere where someone stuck something sharp into me. I did not like that at all and was happy to get back to the place with the familiar smells and sounds.

Not long after this last one left, someone else moved in and – would you believe – this one also has one of my enemies as a pet! I think they shouldn't be allowed in my house. How can anyone like these creatures? A cat is all anyone needs; not only that, we can walk around outside without something or someone attached to us.

Whoever else lives in this big house, just remember this: I'm the one in charge. If I'm outside and want to go in, someone has to bang on the object that opens to let me in. Doesn't happen for the humans.

I like that the humans are my servants – though they don't know it. The only thing is they don't always feed me when I want. You would have thought they'd learned after all this time.

A HOLIDAY WITHOUT MICKEY
By Janet Winson

Lulu had wished for Disneyland this summer. She had wished very hard but now had to accept that it was on hold until next year. No magical castle or breakfast with Pluto or parades and runaway trains. Definitely no late afternoons in a big blue pool shaped liked Mickey's head and ears. Lulu could only think of one word to describe the way she felt that morning, which was 'gutted'. She looked at herself in her bathroom mirror, her expression empty and disappointed. Then she rounded up her special bedtime pals, Elsa and Paddington, and folded them with angry effort into her tiny case on wheels.

"They can't breathe in there," she mumbled, and pushed them in even harder.

There they lay on top of the felt tips, hair bands, new pink nail varnish and the couple of hastily bought comics that Dad had brought upstairs a minute ago. Roughly, she zipped up the case, forcing it closed over one of Elsa's arms, which was trying to escape. Job done, she kicked the case in the direction of the landing at the top of the stairs. She deliberately left the new scrapbook and bottle of glue that Granny had brought round yesterday under her bed. There would definitely be no nice keepsake of the coming awful two weeks in Sidmouth.

Downstairs, Dad looked annoyed as he stood there holding the back door open for her. "Come on, Lulu, you're keeping the boys waiting now." They walked out to his newly purchased Mercedes, with the enormous back seat. "In you go," he said, and quickly clicked her into her seat.

Lulu was squashed into a tiny space on the back seat. Two identical baby seats took up all the room nowadays. Worse still, two non-identical twin brothers were sitting in them, both with blue soothers in their mouths, little bibs round their necks to catch their profuse dribbles. Tom and Rory had arrived two weeks after Christmas, and nothing had felt right since. Nobody listened to Lulu any more. Life itself had become a complete catastrophe, at least according to her.

*

The rented thatched cottage, Stepaside, was a two-minute walk from the beach. Lulu dragged her feet as she waited for the boot to be emptied and reluctantly followed her mum and dad, holding one baby brother each, up to the front door. Lulu instantly noticed the red hollyhocks, almost as tall as herself, in the front garden and the large showing of sunflowers by the gate, which were even taller. When she realised, she was admiring the flowers and being watched she re-set her face in order to let her mouth droop and held the expression as long as she could.

After locating the keys under a flowerpot, they pushed open the big oak door, which creaked as they entered. Lulu noticed how extremely cool it was inside, chilly even. Once her little case emerged, she grabbed it, dashed upstairs to the only bedroom with one single bed and slammed the door. She was hoping for a call from downstairs, but nobody called her; they hadn't even missed her. Lulu sat down on a wide wooden window seat covered in floral cushions, and took in the view into the garden. Disappointed, she realised there was no swing or hot tub, just a bird table and a clay tiled path up to a hidden corner further up.

Elsa and Paddington were propped up on the pillows on the old, high bedstead, which was covered with a cotton throw that matched the cushions and curtains. Lulu approved of the colours in the room, but not enough to make her smile. Next, she began to unpack her t-shirts and shorts and the two 'best dresses' that she was sure would not be needed.

An old Victorian dressing table beside the bed immediately took her attention. She examined it and was pleased to find that the large central mirror and the two smaller side mirrors were all adjustable. With a little effort, she got a good view of the back of her head – and now she actually laughed. She grabbed her hairbrush, which became a microphone, and pretended to be a television presenter.

She stared into the middle mirror and loudly announced, "Here is the local news headlines and weather report for Sidmouth for this weekend." Coughing, she put on a very posh voice and a plastic smile. "The Fishermen's Choir will give a concert tonight at the Parish Church and there will be a sale of walking sticks and mobility buggies in the High Street this weekend. The Vintage Café near the beach will be having a sale of china on Sunday afternoon from 2 p.m. followed by the Friends of Sidmouth Choir singing English folk songs for about an hour." Lulu then faced sideways and said: "Now the weather – it is going to be stifling until next Friday week; sea bathing is banned until further notice due to jellyfish!"

Putting the hairbrush down, Lulu laughed again but also gave the dressing table a hard kick, just to validate her bad mood. As she did so, she caught sight of something moving in the large central mirror. Whatever it was had darted across and then disappeared. Lulu was puzzled but was now feeling thirsty and that was more important to her. All was quiet. The babies were taking their nap and Daddy was catching up on his writing, as he had a deadline to meet with his publisher. So, where was Mummy – and were there any ice cubes to put into a glass of fruit juice?

Lulu found the kitchen downstairs and noticed a sticky-looking bottle of squash. The kettle was recently boiled but there was no sign of cups, biscuits, parents or babies. No sign of any ice cubes in the fridge or the freezer either. Her tummy was rumbling. There was plenty of baby food and milk already in evidence, but little else – and she was hungry. She made some squash in a mug and found half a packet of ready salted crisps, not her favourite at all but she made short work of them anyway.

Proceeding to creep around downstairs, Lulu heard a steady snore and found her dad fast asleep on the sofa, feet up on a stool. He was surrounded by his battered notebook and pens. There were reference books all over the floor, but it was obvious he hadn't even made a start on the important editing.

Lulu climbed onto his lap and loudly yelled straight into the nearest ear. "Wake up, Daddy. I am hungry!"

Paul woke with a start, eyes wild; Lulu was staring at him nose to nose. "I'm very hungry and bored, Daddy. Can we go out and get an ice cream. Now?"

Paul rubbed his eyes and muttered, "Where did that cat come from?"

Hearing this, Lulu wondered if it might have been the tip of a black tail she saw in her mirror earlier. She hoped there really was a cat to play with and started to investigate, but there was no sign of it. Although it was odd, Lulu lost interest and decided to carry on terrorising Daddy.

Before long, they were walking down a path to the beach in the afternoon sun and an ice cream shop was in sight. Things were looking up, but Lulu had a word with herself and stopped smiling when she felt her dad taking a glimpse of her.

"Where are we walking to, Daddy? My feet hurt and I've got a blister. Ouch!!" She gave a yelp of pain and was presented with a Mr. Man plaster from Daddy's wallet; he was well prepared as ever. He had also bought a bucket and spade for Lulu at the shop. Though she hadn't asked for one, he thought it might come in handy.

Lulu dallied by the beach for a while and selected some large flat white pebbles and a few stones to put into the bucket. Walking on, she complained about the weight of the bucket and Daddy ended up carrying it for her.

"Where to now?" she asked, and she gave a loud, long sigh.

"We are looking for a hotel just up the road. I need a photograph – it's for my research."

Lulu felt inquisitive, although she pulled a face. "About Queen Victoria? Did she ever actually come to Sidmouth?"

"She certainly did," Paul said. "She had her very first seaside holiday right here as a very little girl. It was a private house back then but now it's quite a posh hotel. They changed the name to The Sidmouth Beach Hotel and it has a swimming pool outside. When Victoria stayed here it had a German name, 'Pflaume Haus' – it must have had some plum trees in the garden."

"She wasn't actually a Queen then, was she?"

Paul was a moderately successful author and former history teacher who loved to share his knowledge with anyone who seemed even slightly interested. Pleased to see the sudden flicker of interest in Lulu's eyes, he sat on a nearby garden wall, pushed up his glasses and looked hard at his daughter. "Victoria's father died when she was just a baby. Her uncle became King and because he had no children, Victoria was first in line to the throne of England when she was still very young. She grew up in

Kensington Palace in London with her mother and a strict German governess. She was not allowed to do anything on her own, not even walk down the staircase."

Lulu's eyes widened. "Poor Victoria! How horrible for her."

Paul carried on. "Her governess spoke to her in German, and she shared a bedroom with her mother until she was 18 years old."

He could see Lulu was hooked. "I want to see a photo. Did she at least have a pet? Perhaps a dog or a cat?"

Paul was getting a few shots of the hotel now. It stood proud and stoic with a wonderful view of the sea. "If you are a good girl, I'll find some photos for you when we get back and I'll tell you all about Victoria."

Imagination awakened, Lulu became distracted and started to plan a posh tea party with Elsa and Paddington later on in her pretty bedroom with the triple-mirrored dressing table. Paul and Lulu trotted off back towards the cottage and she held her dad's hand, the blister quite forgotten now.

Mum was flustered and trying to make mashed potatoes as Lulu ran into the kitchen. She had Rory on her hip and Tom was screaming blue murder, but she managed to absently pat Lulu on the head and give her a couple of custard creams. "Lulu, can you go and play upstairs until I've sorted dinner out? Daddy wants to do a bit more research before dinner time. You could start a postcard to Granny and we will post it tomorrow."

Lulu pouted and puffed all the way upstairs. "I'm just like poor Victoria. No friends and being ordered about all the time. I hate it here! I want to go home. This is just a boring old house, at a boring seaside." She slammed the door and flopped onto her bed.

She did not recall falling asleep but awoke later to the sound of a cat purring in her ear – or was it? She put her hand out but all she felt was a warm space beside her. "How weird," she thought. "It *must* be that cat again – but where is it now?" She searched under the bed and on the window seat, even in a half-opened drawer. She gave up with a shrug but felt that it was doubly strange as her bedroom door was still firmly shut, just as she had left it. Shrugging again, Lulu wondered if she had actually dreamt it. The cat had certainly left a warm space beside her but now it had disappeared through a closed door.

As she walked past the dressing table and glanced at the middle mirror, she realised her pony tail had come undone and her hair was sticking up at the front. She found her very best hairbrush, which had been a very disappointing Christmas present. Her hair had grown a lot since Christmas and had not been trimmed; it was almost shoulder length. She pushed the brush through her thick locks, yelling when knots presented themselves. As she did so, she noticed the sun had gone down and she drew her bedroom curtains in order to feel cosy and a bit safer. Something just did not feel right.

Lulu thought she caught a glimpse of something in the mirror. Perhaps it was that naughty cat again. It wasn't – but instead, a strange unsmiling woman was there, just head and shoulders, glaring at her. The woman wore a black dress and a white apron; her black hair was parted severely down the middle and her eyes were like matching black beads, not blinking, just staring.

"Oh Louise, my dear. You are a big girl and must now count to a hundred. Yes, a hundred strokes and your hair will shine like a raven's wing. Ein, zwei, drei... and so on, my dear."

Lulu, terrified but transfixed, began to count but the numbers were strange to her, not her language at all. The bristles of the brush were hurting her scalp now. She wanted to shout, "Go away!" but nothing came out.

Tearing herself away from the menacing vision in the mirror, she rushed from the room. Shaken, she ran to find Dad in the kitchen; her scalp, she noticed, was very tender. As she approached him, she suddenly decided to keep what had happened a secret. Surely the frightening vision in the mirror was her imagination? She felt that Mum and Dad would think she was making it up... but she knew she could not sleep alone in that bedroom again. She decided to 'be ill'. She refused her tea, though she was starving, and continued her plan to spend the night in the double bed with Mum and Dad.

Things did not go as she wanted. As usual, the twins kept their parents very busy all evening and Lulu was given some Calpol and sent to bed. Dad came up and read a bedtime story, closed the window and put Lulu's clothes on a chair, which was his usual routine. "Night, night, young lady," he said, not noticing how distracted his daughter was. "I hope you feel better tomorrow. We can have a paddle if it's a nice day." He gave her a kiss, patted Elsa and Paddington and tucked them in. Then he pulled back the curtains a chink. "What a huge moon tonight!" A silver, misty light caught the mirrors. "God bless."

*

Lulu tossed and turned; she could not rid her memory of the woman in the mirror and, once everyone had gone to bed, she felt she could not stay in the room any longer. She found her hairbrush and threw it at the central mirror. The brush hit the target but, being of no weight, it made no noise and landed quietly on the shiny dressing table.

Lulu was shaking as she quietly opened the bedroom door and peeped into the hall. A clock ticked loudly in the downstairs hall and, with a jump, she saw a large, sleeping black cat, his long tail looped around his body. She wished she was brave enough to check whether he was real but instead she lurched back into the bedroom.

Now she could hear the cat purring loudly. She stumbled in the dark, almost falling over the bucket of pebbles just beside her bed. The purring had a strange effect on her and Lulu covered her ears. She was extremely frightened and desperately reached down for two of the biggest pebbles. Moving like a robot, she threw them at the central mirror as hard as she could.

The almighty bang and crash woke everybody. The central mirror was cracked right down the middle; loose shards fell in a deadly pattern on the bedroom carpet, all over the floor. This time, when Lulu opened her mouth, a scream came that was so strong, she felt she had lost her breath and all her strength in one go. She felt herself slipping away…

Lulu found herself in her parents' double bed and heard Dad clearing up the glass in her own bedroom, carefully wrapping the larger pieces in the double pages of his *Daily Telegraph* and then hoovering up the rest. After another spoonful of Calpol, Lulu was cuddled to sleep, with no questions asked. That could wait until the morning.

Lulu slept fitfully. As soon as dawn crept into the big bedroom, she grabbed Paddington and Elsa and slid away from

Mum's side of the bed while her parents slept. Creeping downstairs, she climbed onto the big leather recliner. She started to worry about how much trouble she was in and whether everything had been a dream – but her scalp was still smarting and her stomach was doing somersaults. She remembered the image of the shards of broken glass and crossed her fingers that the dressing table would be removed now, yet – with surprise – she realised it had all been something of a thrill, despite the terror that had followed. It had been very frightening but also exciting, in a way.

Meanwhile, her mum and dad were waking up both a little the worse for wear. Recalling the events of the night before left them worried and confused. Mum reluctantly started the conversation.

"Lulu has acted so strangely since we got here, Paul. She has been spending too much time alone in that bedroom. We've not really had more than a couple of words out of her and she just ignores the twins. What on earth is going on?"

Paul found his glasses and, after rubbing his eyes, put them on. He looked very miserable. "Lulu has been increasingly difficult since Tom and Rory arrived. I was hoping this break would cheer her up but look what's happened now. We need to get home and try to find out what is going on in her mind. We know she can be difficult, but something has happened in the cottage to really terrify her." He paused. "First things first, I 'd better find the caretaker's number to report the damage. I wonder if they will refuse to return our deposit? I just hope that bedroom furniture was junk shop stuff, not antique or anything. What's more, how are we going to explain any of this?"

Downstairs, Lulu had found an appetite and was feeling well enough to request a bacon sandwich for breakfast, which she ate very quickly. "I like this recliner, Daddy. Can I please sleep down here until we go home on Saturday? That dressing table upstairs is haunted. That's why I smashed it up."

With difficulty, Paul kept a straight face. "Mummy and I think you're unhappy, Lulu. What you did was for attention, right? We need to sort everything out – we can't have you deliberately destroying things like that."

"That lady in the mirror made me do it, Daddy! She was so horrible. She hated me. She might have hurt Rory and Tom, too." Lulu went on to describe the face in the mirror, the black unblinking eyes and the hair-brushing ritual. "She knew my real name, Daddy! She called me Louise. I think she was real."

"I think we had better go home, Lulu. I need to ring the caretaker to let him know about the damage and that we are leaving today instead of Saturday. Mummy will be down with the boys in a minute."

Lulu wouldn't go back into the bedroom but stayed in her pyjamas in front of the TV with Elsa and Paddington, one each side of her, under a blanket that made a great tent to feel safe inside.

*

Joe Bruce, the caretaker, took Paul's message very calmly and promised to pop in shortly. When he did, Paul made him a cup of coffee and then showed him the state of the dressing table.

Joe was a middle-aged man who took everything in his stride and didn't ask questions. He looked at Paul in a sympathetic way and said they would need to remove the dressing table and give the bedroom a very thorough clean, just in case there were remains of glass splinters in the carpet.

Just before he left, he turned to Paul and said: "I saw you and your little girl the other day taking photos down at the Sidmouth Beach Hotel. I've heard it's been sold on yet again. Did anyone mention it?"

"I'm a writer, Joe, and I have been researching my new book. It's about Queen Victoria's favourite holiday places. I was down in the Isle of Wight last month, and here in Sidmouth now. I'm running out of time – my intention is to be ready to publish in time for this Christmas."

A little spark of interest changed Joe's expression. "Of course, you must be aware that hotel was once a private home where Victoria spent her first seaside holiday. It's had a variety of different owners over the last 60 years or so. I've lived locally for the past 30-odd years. In fact, this little cottage, Stepaside was full of the original furniture from the big house, ever since a big revamp in the 1970s. That big old dressing table must be the last large piece of that furniture from an auction back then. There are also a few little bookcases and a couple of side tables downstairs somewhere. I reckon the owners will get the dressing table fixed. It has provenance; there will be paperwork somewhere. They'll get a local glazier to sort it out."

Paul shook hands with Joe. "We've loved the cottage but that back bedroom has a bad vibe, Joe. Has anyone mentioned it before?"

Joe laughed. He looked a little red in the face. "Did you see the black cat, too? It's something that puzzles me. If it is a stray, it must be in its dotage by now. Royalty usually have dogs or race horses, not cats! Yes, it's a spooky old place."

Paul was speechless as he opened the door for Joe, who gave him a quick wave and shut the front gate.

THE SNAKE CATCHER
By Julia Gale

We were sitting in our local public house in the New Forest, enjoying a few drinks by the fireside, my wife and I, seeing in the new century. We chatted about life and the changes we have seen over the years; believe me, there have been many – the motor car and electricity, for instance. We wondered what other changes the twentieth century would bring. We'd had a few drinks, so that may have been why my wife suddenly came up with this idea.

'Josiah,' she said, 'why don't you a write a journal about the time you were a snake catcher? I'm sure people in the future will be interested; it's a dying trade in this country, snake catching.'

I nodded in agreement. 'It is that. But how is an illiterate old man like me going to keep a journal, and who would be interested in reading it anyway?' I asked. Though I rather liked the idea of someone in the future reading about me.

'That's easy,' she replied. 'We just ask Alex if he would be willing to do the writing for you. He's good with words – he did go to school, you know.'

I'd almost forgotten that.

Before I could answer her, who should appear but the very same – Alex, my wife's adopted son. I suppose he is mine now, too, which pleases me. I told him about our idea, and he agreed to help me – as long as I included him, his mother and my good old horse Bess in the story.

I also need to mention my encounter with a reporter, who came all the way down from "the Smoke" – that's what we locals call our fair capital in this part of the country – just to speak to me. After all, it did change my life eventually.

'Probably best to write it in the present tense,' Alex suggested. I wasn't quite sure what he meant. Alex explained that it would look as if I was writing down everything there and then. I was happy with that. 'It may take us quite a long time,' he said.

'I have all the time in the world, son. Let us do this.'

As he turned to reply, Alex had a strange expression on his face. I then realised I'd called him "son" for the first time...

'Yes, Dad.' He smiled. 'And who knows, you may become famous after this...?'

*

My name is Josiah Brown and I am writing this journal in the year 1890.

I am a snake catcher by trade. Let's see – a sort of pest controller would be the best way of describing what I do. Of course, I have not always done this type of work. I've had many different jobs before, but some years ago my life was hit with major tragedy and hard times came upon me. I was forced to live the life of a hermit, off the land and foraging for food. Not that I mind in the least; I've always been a bit of a loner. My home is a shack made of wood and mud, which I built with my own hands. It's not comfortable and it's very cold in the winter, but at least it provides me with a bit of shelter. A snake catcher's life is not an easy one; I rise with the dawn and go to bed at sunset. My horse Bess and I are out in all weathers, twelve months a year.

In the mornings, one of the first things I do is put a saddle on Bess and attach her to my cart. Then we set off to work. I always make sure I carry my pitchfork and net with me. People often tell me I should wear special gloves as the creatures can get quite vicious at times, especially the ones that don't want to get caught – which is all of them, of course. However, I've not been bitten once yet, and I've been doing this for a good few years now.

Bess and I walk for miles each day, going from village to village in search of them wrigglers. I call the snakes I catch "wrigglers" because of the way they wriggle on my fork, before I put them into my sack.

Hunting for snakes can make me quite a large sum of money, especially in the summer months. Snakes are at their most lively then and that is when I'm likely to get the most customers, villagers mainly, needing help in ridding their properties of the reptiles. The little devils slither into their houses when nobody is looking and then they curl up in cupboards and fireplaces, scaring housewives, children and business people alike, once they have been discovered. I willingly help them all, knowing full well they will pay me a good price for my services.

At the end of the day, Bess and I make our way to The Railway Inn, where my good friend Mary is the landlady. She usually has a homemade meal ready for me, alongside a glass or two of local cider.

When I'm not getting rid of people's reptile problems, I go searching through the many gorse bushes in this area for the creatures. Then I take them home and boil them down to make anti-venom and other ointments. I learnt how to make remedies for different ailments from my mother. She was well known in the village where we lived; she was a herbalist and people came from near and far for her medicines. In the winter months snakes hibernate, and business is very poor. That's when I take my anti-venom and ointments to the local markets to sell. Sometimes I am successful in selling my wares, and at other times sales are poor. It's a hard time of year for Bess and me. I struggle to make ends meet, and we are grateful to have a friend like Mary, who often takes us in (Bess in the stable) if the weather is very cold.

We aren't getting any younger, though I don't know my exact age. Mary tells me she is fast approaching fifty, so I must be about the same age, judging from the wrinkles on my brown skin, baked in the sun, and my somewhat fat stomach and bushy, grey beard.

Every so often, I go with my catches up to London by train, leaving Bess behind, of course. I take them to the new zoo up there. They feed my snakes to their birds of prey; the zookeeper, Jack, is a goodly fellow and pays me handsomely. Jack and I have started to get to know each other quite well; I'd call him a friend, even. He once tried to persuade me to move up there and offered me a job of work at the zoo, cleaning out the animal cages. I politely turned his offer down. I don't like London; it's noisy and smelly. Give me the New Forest, always. It's my home and that is where I am going to stay.

As it happens, Jack is a good friend of Sir Charles Braddock. Sir Charles is the squire of Lyndhurst Manor and the local Member of Parliament for the New Forest. His family and mine go back a long way in history, it might surprise you. We have not always had the best of relationships though. It was, however,

Sir Charles who helped me get the job in London, for the reasons I give below. He has to travel a lot between his two homes, here in the forest and London; I think that's how he met Jack. It's an unlikely friendship, to be sure.

Here's a thing. I once saved Sir Charles's son Arthur's life with one of my ant-venom solutions. Arthur was out riding with his father one day, fell from his horse and the poor boy got bitten by a snake, who'd been terrified itself, of course, and struck out.

There aren't many doctors who live near Lyndhurst Manor. So, Sir Charles sent one of his servants out to look for me and I did my best for him. Sir Charles was so delighted by his son's recovery that he promised he would make my act of kindness and my medicines known across the capital and beyond. It sparked a barrage of interest in me and the news soon caught the interest of the newspapers. The story caught the eye of one reporter in particular; so much so that he travelled all the way down here just to interview me.

*

The day this reporter arrived I was caught by surprise. Bess and I had had a bad day out by the gorse bushes and we decided to return home early. It was late autumn and very cold. I had not caught much, not enough to take up to London the next day, anyhow. I decided to take the shortest route home as it was beginning to get dark, though it was only about 4 p.m. in the afternoon. I walked beside my Bess; she has arthritis and cannot load-bear very well now. It took us a fair while to get back and we were very cold and hungry by the time we arrived at the inn.

I spotted Alexander running towards us. Bess was pleased to see him; she likes Alex and he spoils her with treats. Alex is around eighteen, about the same age as my son would have been, and often I imagine the two of them growing up together, just as Mary and I did.

'I'll take Bess to the stables. It looks like you have a visitor and are going to have a long night, Josiah,' Alex said, once he had caught his breath.

I turned around to ask him what he meant, but he had already started to make his way back to the stable with Bess. That boy can move fast when he wants to! I thought about what he had said: a visitor? I never get any visitors, except for one time I fell afoul of the law; even then I saw the copper off pretty quickly.

I pushed open the door of the inn, which was fuller than usual for a Thursday evening. A load of sailors on shore leave from Southampton had made their way here by train and were spending their wages on beer, tobacco and their newly acquired "lady friends" from the dockside. They are frequent visitors to Mary's pub and on occasion ask Mary if she has a room to spare; she always turns them away. I don't like them myself – much too rowdy. I looked around for Mary, but she was nowhere to be seen.

Feeling uncomfortable, I had just started to make my way back to the door when a tall, elegant-looking gentleman wearing an expensive suit, a long overcoat and a top hat tapped me on the shoulder. 'I say, old man, are you Josiah Brown?' he asked.

'It depends who's asking. You're not the law, are you?' I replied, defensively.

He stood there smiling as he answered my question. 'Oh no, old boy, nothing like that. My name is Oliver Prendergast and I am a reporter for the Times newspaper in London. I have been sent down here to write an article about life in the country and about people of interest who live there. You see, many people are talking about you and your miracle cures; they have sparked a lot of curiosity about you and your lifestyle. My good friend Charles Braddock told me he is acquainted with you and that your families go back a long way. He also told me I would have a hard job getting any information from you.' He smiled when he said this, so I wouldn't take offence. 'He told me about the way you saved his son after an accident. Could you spare me some of your time? You will be well rewarded, I promise you.'

Instinctively, I felt that I wanted to be alone. The situation made me feel uncomfortable and unsure what to do. The thing is, although Sr Charles felt he owed me something, I knew he wasn't too happy about my connection with his sister – I'll tell you more later. Do I let this man do his interview or do I ask him to get his things and go? But this reporter fellow was obviously not going to leave me alone; after all, he had travelled a fair distance just to speak to me. I decided to give him what he wanted, just so I could be rid of him quickly and have my dinner.

'Okay, I'll talk to you, but on my terms only. When Mary comes with my food you scarper back to where you came from, understand?'

He nodded in agreement. 'I understand,' he said.

I led him through the crowded pub to the spot where I usually sit, in the corner near the fireplace. Thankfully, it was unoccupied. We sat down, and after Oliver paid for a drink each we began.

Prendergast took his notebook and a fancy ink pen out of his bag. He hesitated. 'I must confess, old man, that this is the first time I've done this type of interview on my own. I'm new to the job, you see,' he explained, nervously. 'But...nothing ventured, eh? I'll start at the beginning – always a good place. Where and when were you born, Josiah?'

Before answering him, I took a last swig of my cider and lit my pipe with a taper. After that, I began to feel a little more comfortable, and ready to answer his questions.

'I was born in the year of our Lord, 1840 or thereabouts, not sure exactly when. But I know for sure that I was born on Sir Charles's estate, in the labourer's cottage there; my father worked as a general labourer and handyman for many years, you see? I am the youngest of four children, sadly all gone now. My mother made and sold herbal remedies; she taught me everything I know. You see, none of us went to school. I still can't read or write.'

'Oh, so you are illiterate then? Are all the country folk in the New Forest unschooled?' Prendergast asked. I wasn't sure whether he was being sarcastic.

'How should I know? Go and ask your friend Sir Charles,' I replied, sharply. I had taken a sudden dislike to the man.

'No need to take it like that, old man. Just being curious. It's my job.'

It took the offer of another drink before I was prepared to speak to him again.

*

'Shall we start again? I really would like to hear more.'

We finished our drinks in silence whilst I thought about it. To be honest, I was beginning to get a little bored with the whole situation, but the couple of drinks I'd had earlier were starting to loosen my tongue.

Finally, I said, 'Go on then...but I'll tell the story my way – you say nothing, Prendergast, have I made myself clear? And if I hear you call me an old man one more time I'll throw you out personally, never mind what Mary or anyone else thinks. Understood?'

As he sat down once more in silence, Prendergast suddenly looked younger than his years, and a bit vulnerable.

'You already know where and when I was born, so no need to go over it all again, is there?' Prendergast shook his head. I continued my story from where I left off.

'Sir Horace, Sir Charles' father, was a good man, and kind. – or so I thought. He let my family live in the cottage rent free, unlike the other servants who had to pay rent for their houses out of their wages. I didn't get to know the real reason why he showed us such favour until much later on...

'As we grew up and became old enough to work, my brother and I also became labourers on the estate. My two sisters went into the house and became maids to his wife, Lady Maria. She was a kindly woman, but very poor in health. They had three children, Charles, James and Martha. Lady Maria passed away when Charles was around fifteen years of age. My two sisters soon left to seek other employment. This left Horace to bring up the three children alone, although of course he employed governesses and nannies for them, but they never seemed to stay long for some reason. Whenever one of the children became ill, Horace would ask for my mother to bring her medicines and nurse them. Why he didn't make use of the village doctor, I'll probably never know. Occasionally, Mother was called upon to stay at the manor house overnight, sometimes for many nights in a row. Sir Horace was strict like that. Mother would always return from her nursemaid duties worn out and upset. I remember my father at one time becoming very angry with Horace for making my mother work so hard. Maybe Sir Horace wasn't such a good man after all.

'My mother became very ill and died; neither medicine nor any of her own potions could cure her. Horace suddenly no longer required my father's services and dismissed him. He went to live with my sister, Doris. My brother Frank and I, however, stayed on to work on the estate. Frank eventually became a butler in the main house, and I was made chief labourer and grounds man. I was extremely contented and always made sure I worked hard.

'A few years later, when Horace died, he left the now adult Charles in charge of the estate. Charles was very different from his father and took a particular dislike to me, especially as I had now begun to take an interest in his sister, Martha.

'Martha was a pretty girl with blonde hair in ringlets, a fair complexion and sapphire eyes that lit up the room whenever she entered. Of course, I first knew Martha when she was a lot younger, but as soon as she was old enough, she was sent away to boarding school; none of us saw much of her during that time. She came home for holidays, of course, but her days playing on her own in the fields were over.

'Soon after her father passed away, Martha returned home, now a young woman of eighteen. That is when I began to notice her for the first time. She would come out every day to the fields with lunch for all those who worked on the estate. It was not seemly for the lady of the house to mingle with the servants, but she didn't seem to care much for etiquette. She was very different from either of her two brothers.

'Before long, we started to become friends and that friendship soon developed into romance. Martha didn't seem notice the ten-year age difference between us. We began to meet each other in secret, often hiding in different locations within the grounds, hoping we'd never be caught; each of us knew there would be serious consequences if we were.

'Such secrecy could not last, and we were found out by one of the other servants. Unbeknown to us, Martha's brothers had become suspicious of the two of us and our friendship and had employed them to spy on us. Once he found us, he instantly reported us back to the brothers. They were enraged and ordered me up to the house. I knew it could mean instant dismissal, but as long as I still had Martha I felt I could face anything.

However, would Martha feel the same about me? I was just glad my brother Jack was no longer working there to witness this.

'The meeting went every bit as badly as I had imagined. They were both extremely angry and used hate-filled words the like of which I never wish to hear again. They banished me from the house, the estate and my work. Just as I turned to leave the room, the brothers dropped their final bombshell. They told me they had discovered some letters their father had written to my mother. The letters begged my mother to keep quiet about their affair!

'Sir Horace had offered her money to be rid of the baby she was having. My mother obviously didn't take it. The letters were written a few months before I was born, so it took little working out to see that made me their illegitimate half-brother!

'I did not think I would be welcomed into the family – and I was right. The word "affair" never rang aright with me; it seemed to indicate love and mutual respect. Perhaps she loved *him* – but when I think of how Mother often came home tearful and exhausted, I can only feel that he used her to the last.

'Within a day I had gathered my few belongings from the only home I had ever known, heartbroken at the thought of my mother's affair, betrayed and frightened for my future. I walked down the drive for the final time, knowing that I would, and should, never see Martha again. Would they tell her?

'Martha stood at the end of the path, waiting. She held out her hand. I looked curiously at her and realised she was unaware of who I was. But if you ask me why the brothers never told her, I would not be able to tell you – I think shame and fear of scandal may explain it.

'We moved away from Lyndhurst Manor and the memories. We settled in Brockenhurst and married soon afterwards, a small ceremony in the village church. We found a tiny cottage to live in. It was a far cry from the life Martha was used to, but she adapted amazingly to the hardship of working country life. I taught her everything I knew about wild plants and herbs and how to make lotions and medicine from them, just as my mother had done all those years before. I worked as a casual labourer on a nearby farm. We made do with what we had and were happy together.

'What I did was wrong – I make no bones about it. Martha never found out we were half siblings; I never told her. God will judge me for what I have done. I can only say that I did my best to make her happy – but the tragedies that followed make me think God has already made up his mind.

'A couple of years later, Martha gave birth to a baby boy; we named him Daniel and Martha died of illness brought on by childbirth a few days later. The lordly brothers wanted nothing to do with their nephew and I was left to bring up Daniel by myself. Again, I turned to Mary for help, even though she was inexperienced with children herself.

'As he grew older, I taught Daniel how to live off the land and to make medicines, just as I had with his mother. He was a quick learner and before he was ten was helping me in the fields, something he loved to do – but even the happiness of this togetherness was denied. One day, cutting a gorse bush, he disturbed a sleeping adder, which bit him. I managed to walk him home and treated the bite with one of my potions, but could not save him.

'Again, I was left heartbroken and alone. That is when I decided I would rid the forest of all reptiles. That decision was made out of anger over what had been taken away from me, but also so that no one else would ever have to lose a loved one in this way. I became the one and only snake-catcher in these parts.

'I sold the cottage and moved into a shack in the middle of the woods. I'd had enough of the follies and hate of others, so I bought a horse for company, an animal I feel has more loyalty and sense than many humans. It took some time before I let Mary persuade me into accepting help, and she began cooking for me most evenings.'

At this point, I noticed Prendergast had stopped writing. He was looking at me, not unkindly I felt, and I could see he was thinking hard about all that I had said.

'What say you, then, Mr. Prendergast? Is it God or your readership that should judge me?'

He sighed, and put his pen and paper away. Finally, he smiled. 'I think God has more experience in these matters than either I or my readership,' he said.

51

I rose and shook his hand. Then I gathered Bess up outside and went back to my shack in the woods.

*

The years have passed and much has happened since the reporter's visit. I never heard of my story being printed in the paper.

I continued to hunt snakes and live in my wooden shack, until it was vandalised by a group of local youths. I managed to rebuild it again, only for it to be vandalised again, which was enough for me. I became so unwell and worn that Mary took me to live with her and Alex permanently. Eventually, I made Mary my wife; we sold The Railway Inn for a much smaller public house, which Alex now owns. He has named it The Snake Catcher's Arms.

SPACE AND TIME
(A poem for Jan)
By Richie Stress

Our love, it feels like fireflies

That light their way to my heart

A choir of fluttering butterflies

They tell us never to part

A love woven within the fabric

of space and of time -

A fabric made of vicuna wool

and mulberry silk lined and signed inside:

one love, one life, one body and one mind.

ETERNITY RISING
By C.G. Harris

The stars are bright tonight; I mean, really bright. I was on the way to class but people were standing in the streets looking up, and if I hadn't been in a hurry I'd have stopped with them. The moon was dazzling too; not bigger, not closer, just glowing as if it wanted to keep up with its heavenly neighbours.

Old Taylor's class is very good; I don't like to miss any of it. He's got a way with him, has Taylor. Philosophy, see? Dry subject, but he brings it alive and he's always got a new take on things – it's not just your Plato or your Aristotle, though I'm alright with them, and the Stoics as well – and I like new ideas. I fancy myself open to anything. If somebody wants to say something, I'll consider it. I'll chew it over and I'll give it my best shot at a thought or two – and I surprise a few people, I think; we're not all thick in South London.

I sit down in my usual seat, near the back, with the window to my side. In the summer, with the long evenings, it's lovely having a bit of sunlight warming you up and dancing around on the walls, like my thoughts; in the winter, like now, when the evenings are cold and tight and drawn, I can see the street lights all in a row. They look really feeble right now, up against those stars.

Taylor normally ambles in a few minutes late, but tonight... Well, I wouldn't say he is hurrying exactly but he's not ambling, He's frowning a bit, and preoccupied. When he throws his folders on the table we all sit up, about a dozen of us; he's got our attention. I reckon he's got something new to tell us – we were due a talk on ethics, but he's pushed that lot aside. This could be more interesting.

I was right. He's pushed that floppy fringe away from his forehead, sat on the desk with his legs crossed and let at us. At first, I'm thinking he's going down the Solipsism route. That's not new at all – that the only thing that exists, that we can be sure exists, is the *self.* That is, only my thoughts exist; the rest of it, the so-called *reality*, isn't really there at all. He slings in a bit of Descartes as well, like how do I know *I* exist? Well, in a nutshell, old Descartes says: *"I think, therefore I am."*

He starts in on the old *"We are the centre of the universe"* thing, then realises he's not making a good job of this, so he stops and starts again, slowly. He looks at us all – strangely, I think. "Listen," he says. "What if we have been created, *all* been created to kill a bit of time...a *lot* of time? Not us alone...but everything." He nods at the window. "All of it."

I look out of the window at that; we all do. I'm feeling a bit cold inside now because I can't quite see where this is going, but I don't think I like it really. And the stars look a bit dimmer than they did; I don't like that either.

The good-looking blonde in the front row puts her hand up. She's got brains, that one; I didn't want her to be a stereotype so I made... I shake my head hard a few times and concentrate on what she is saying.

"You mean, Mr. Taylor, that we're an amusement?" she says.

"No," he says, instantly, "no, not an amusement..." He shakes his head hard, just like I did. "I would say, a necessity."

I put up my hand. "I'm not following you, Mr. Taylor," I say, though something is creeping its way into my brain. No, not my brain, my mind, my...*me*.

Taylor pushes back his fringe again, then gets up and paces to and fro.

"Imagine," he says, "Eternity. Capital 'E'. Go on."

We all try. We sit, some with eyes closed, others with eyes to the ceiling, imagining.

It's horrifying.

Endless. Timeless. Foreverness.

The stars are paler now, I notice. "Go on," I say, quietly, to Mr. Taylor. And we all lean forward in our seats.

"Think of Nothingness. You are all there is, whatever *you* are. Nothing to look forward to, or look back on. Only...Nothing." It's coming thick and fast now, and he paces more quickly. "What would you do, if you could?"

Some are shaking their heads hard now. Not everybody, not yet.

There's a bloke in the front row, short hair and shiny eyes. He pipes up:

"It's obvious, isn't it? I'd make something up, something to keep me occupied." He stops a moment, then continues. "Things. Important, unimportant. Emotions; happy, sad, angry; whatever emotion I could make up. Things to put those emotions in. And other things to enable them to think about those emotions. Puzzles, questions. The means to find out the answers – but not all of them. Things to look at and wonder at. Small things to peer at through microscopes. Big things to look up at. Huge things: stars, galaxies, the Universe…universes…"

"Things to give you purpose," says Mr. Taylor.

"Things to stop you getting bored," says the blonde.

"And lonely," I whisper.

They all look at me and they are all shaking their heads now because they don't want to remember. *We* don't want to remember. *I* don't want to remember.

Taylor comes over to me and sits down. "You can only hold back remembering so long. It killed a few billion years this time, didn't it? And a few billion the time before that. And before that, well, millions or billions, and before that…and before that…"

There's a hunter in the Serengeti thinking the same. And an Inuit in Alaska, a Hindi in Gujarat and a Muscovite wrapped in fur. A cowboy in a Stetson herding cattle in a dustbowl. A politician rising to speak in the Commons and a woman on the catwalk. A worker, fitting headlights on a Ford and a child folding paper in Japan. A wave in the sea and a wind in the trees. A raindrop on a leaf.

A tsunami of unwilling remembrance.

The bloke with the shiny nose has vanished, and the rest of the class now too. The blonde with the brains smiled at me; she was a favourite of mine, before she went. Only Taylor and I remain. The moon no longer hangs in the sky and, quietly, we watch the stars blink out, one by one.

"I'm frightened, Mr. Taylor," I whisper.

I know he would have put his hand in mine, if he existed, but Nothingness came upon me once more, then:

"Let There Be Light!" I say yet again.

THERE'S NO MYSTERY HERE
By Tony Ormerod

The Secretary,
British Union of Fascists

3rd November 1936

Dear Sir,

I hardly know whether to thank you or despise you for the letter I have recently received. You have sadly misjudged me if you think I have any intention of taking up the invitation to speak at your next meeting, or should I more accurately describe it as a rally?

I cannot begin to imagine why you think I would make a suitable candidate to address your 'Blackshirts'. You must know that one of my closest friends, a well-known and respected detective, was a victim of the Hun during the Great War; his cruel experiences as a refugee of poor little Belgium have made him naturally suspicious of any organisation with any kind of link to the New Germany. His sound advice is that I should distance myself from you and your rather shady colleagues but, as I have informed him, he is preaching to the converted.

Jane, another close, dear friend, shares my views. A lovely, quaint lady, she also suffered when she lost her fiancé in 1916; another victim of Prussian aggression. Jane is someone who, in spite of living off the beaten track, can always be relied on to dispense sound advice based on an uncanny knowledge of human nature.

High hopes for your leader Oswald Moseley when he broke away from the main political parties have been dashed as far as I am concerned. Foolish man. Having chosen the wrong path, he has turned into a bullying braggart, a mere leader of thugs. Mark my words, it will all end in tears. That aside, black just does not suit me; it ages one so.

In the hope that everything goes badly for you, I remain your intractable foe,

Agatha Christie

MOLLY MAC'S BIRTHDAY
By JULIA GALE

'Wake up Mol, it's gone ten o clock and we have a busy day ahead. It's your birthday' remember?"

Slowly, I opened my eyes to find Sarah, one of the carers at Pleasant View Nursing Home, leaning over my bed with a silly grin on her face.

I had been having a lovely dream about my late husband, Norman, one of many about him in recent months, and really was not happy at being woken up.

'What do you mean I've got I have a busy day ahead? Surely, I'm the one who decides how busy my day is going to be, not you or the other staff? Really, you should know that by now, silly girl.'

I regretted my brusqueness straightaway - I hadn't meant to snap at her like that, but I really wasn't feeling quite myself that day.

'Are you alright Mol, you look ever so pale? Because if you are feeling unwell, it's my duty to tell, the nurse; she'll call the doctor for you, just to give you a check over.'

In the whole of the twenty-five years of living here, never had I required a doctor to call on me. I was quite proud of the fact that in all those years I'd had nothing more than the common cold.

'The day you call the doctor, will be the day I'm on my death bed, understood?' I snapped again. Sarah nodded her head to show me that she understood alright.

'I'll go downstairs and get your breakfast shall I'? For some reason, she sounded as if she was about to cry.

I really didn't mean to upset her, after all she was in my opinion the best carer the home had employed for a long time. Also, I really didn't mind her calling me Mol, actually found her informal approach to me quite refreshing, I had become very fond of Sarah over the years. She had become my favourite, often taking the time after her long shift to sit and talk to me. The other staff never bothered to do so, they were so busy or seemed to be. She always listened with interest and even fascination to my stories about Norman's acting career and my early days as a dancer for the Royal Ballet.

A few minutes later, Sarah reappeared with my breakfast tray; in the centre was a tiny vase with a single rose in it. Sarah placed the tray on the table by the window. Normally I ate my meals looking out of the window, watching the world go by. But today I felt too weak to move.

'I think I'll have my breakfast in bed today, if you don't mind'' I said.

Sarah looked worried as she bought the tray and placed it on the bed, and then helped me sit up. I struggled to eat my soft-boiled egg and bread soldiers, even the tea made me choke.

'Are you sure that you are ok, Mol'? Sarah asked again, as she picked up the plates, cup and cutlery that were now scattered across my bed.

'I feel fine dear, just feeling my age I suppose. Now tell me about the plan for the rest of the day, you know how I hate surprises.'

To be honest up to this point I had all but forgotten my birthday. After all who wants to celebrate becoming 103? I most certainly did not. but had to find a way to distract Sarah from worrying about my worsening state of health. She did not look convinced by my response to her question.

She sat on the edge of the bed, and spoke in a quiet tone

'Well, I'm not really meant to tell you this but, they have arranged for the BBC to come and have a little chat with you. Because not only is it your birthday, it is also exactly twenty-five years to the day since you arrived here.'

I knew that already, but was not keen to make a big deal out of it, myself.

'I'd like to get hold of the little so and so that leaked that little gem'. I thought to myself.

'I think that the BBC are planning to record you this afternoon and broadcasting it on one of their morning news shows - isn't that exciting Mol?'

I gave her my best smile, but I was feeling everything but excitement. She also told me that a big afternoon tea was planned to honour my birthday, they had planned the party for my 100th, but had to cancel because of the pandemic.

The whole idea seemed horrendous to me, if there was anything I disliked more than secrets it was being made a fuss of., but it seemed I really didn't have a choice.

'What time does all this start?' I asked.

'The BBC are arriving around 2ish I think.'

'Good, that gives me some time to rest and prepare myself, doesn't it?' I asked Sarah.

'Not much' she said, looking at her watch. 'I'll be back in an hour.'

I smiled. 'Ok then.'

I lay my head on the pillow, and let my mind wander back to the day I first met Norman.

*

The summer of 1946 was a particularly drab and wet one as I recall. My friend and flat mate, Janice and I, were celebrating the start of our first season as professional dancers with the Royal Ballet Company. It was also my twenty-first birthday. We decided to celebrate in style with an afternoon tea at the Ritz.

The restaurant was crowded when we arrived; it remained that way until we were almost ready to leave. As we were finishing up dessert, a guilty pleasure, bearing in mind that we were now wafer-thin professional dancers and expected to remain so, in walked a man. Is it possible to see someone for the first time and know that, rightly or wrongly you are destined to be together? I would not have thought so, until that moment.

He was tall, neatly and strikingly dressed in a suit that could only have been purchased from Saville Row; he wore a brightly coloured cravat around his neck. The waiter took his coat and umbrella and ushered him to the table next to ours. I could not help but notice him looking in our direction.

'I'll bet he's got a bit of money; I swear that he was in a film I've seen recently.' Janice whispered to me. I affected nonchalance and shrugged my shoulders.

The man ordered food from the menu and drank red wine whilst waiting for his meal to arrive; it seemed to me that he drank a glass more than was necessary and when he stood and walked towards to our table, I was convinced of it. Yet, something pleased me about the fact he was coming this way, wine or no, rather than walking towards the exit in the opposite direction, perhaps never to be seen again,

His face was flushed a little but I believe this was with embarrassment rather than the effects of the wine. Janice almost giggled when he stood before us and inclined his head in a slight old-fashioned bow; for myself I was silent and thought he was the most beautiful man I had ever seen.

'I, err, I...excuse me ladies.' he said. 'I do hope you don't think that I'm not being too forward? But I have only just moved to London. This is outrageous of me I'm sure but...well...I...I'm looking for a couple of companions to help me become-acquainted with the city?' We must have looked as startled as we felt and he rushed on rather calamitously.

'Don't worry ladies, I will pay you...no, that...I mean I don't want anything more from you, I'm a married man. I have a wife and daughter.' He quickly showed us his wedding ring, but that didn't provide much reassurance. It was then that he realised things were not going well and he sighed. He reached inside his jacket pocket and pulled out a small calling card. It was embossed and had his name and telephone number upon it. He handed it to us. He sighed again at our silence, shook his head and said:

'Please, have a think about it ladies.' He then went back to his table and his wine.

We called for the bill, asked for our coats, and resisted the urge to run out of the restaurant – one did not run in the Ritz. I'm not sure whether we were shocked by our encounter or not. Janice, I felt, was constantly on the verge of laughing, whilst my own thoughts were of the warnings my mother had given me about strangers before I moved to London from the midlands. If he was really married, why then hadn't he asked us to show them around as well?

As soon as we arrived back at our shared apartment, I tore the card to with his telephone number on it into little pieces threw them in the bin. Janice tried to stop me. 'Now, don't be hasty!' she laughed. But it was too late – although I made sure that I read his name first:

Norman Staunton.

*

It was only two weeks before I saw him again. I was about to board a train at Victoria station and I felt a tentative tap me on the back. I turned and it was he. To my horror, or was it excitement - he also got into the same carriage as me. The carriage was pretty full,

'At least I'll be able to get help should I need it.' I thought, as I sat on one of two vacant seats. He sat next to me; I could feel his closeness.

'You *are* one of the young ladies I had the pleasure of meeting in the Ritz a while ago, aren't you?' he said.

'Y, yes, I am,' I stumbled with my words. 'How did you recognise me?' I asked.

He smiled and told me that he didn't forget a pretty face easily.

'Look, I didn't leave you or your friend with a very good impression, did I?'

'No, you didn't we were terrified.' I replied.

'Really? Well, yes you both looked like a pair of rabbits about to go into a pie' he said. We both laughed at that.

'Please let me explain, for I am truly sorry,' And so it began. Romance. Of a sort – and with a married man at the time no less. I accepted his explanation that he had returned to England from America just a just a couple of days before he came into the Ritz, and that he had been feeling lonely being separated from his wife and daughter. I raised my eyebrows at that. 'Oh, please don't get me wrong, my wife and I are divorcing and I am seeking custody of my daughter – but loneliness is a terrible thing when you are used to being with someone you care about.' I nodded. I think I understood.

'Then I saw the two of you, and thought that you both looked like the sort of people I could be friends with. It was only after I got home that I fully realised what I'd said and

63

done. I'd been hoping for an opportunity to see one or both of you again, and have a chance to apologise.'

I accepted his apology, though I still felt uneasy. He told me that he wanted to make amends by taking me for something to eat.

'You mean "us"?' I asked, thinking of Janice. He placed his hand lightly upon mine. I mean you, he said quietly. He gave me another calling card – I told him that I had mislaid his earlier one I had not the heart to tell him I had torn it up.

'My name is…'

'Norman' I said.

He smiled,

'And yours?'

'Molly McQuinn' I replied.

'Pretty name, Norman said. I felt myself blush.

I got off the train one stop early and walked home, not really quite sure of what had just happened on the train. Janice was out with her boyfriend when I arrived home. So, I made a quick supper and went to bed; this time I put Norman's number in a draw by my bedside.

I did wonder what my parents would make of my strange encounter with Norman.

*

I think when love overtakes you caution can go out of the window. A couple of days later, I managed to find the courage to telephone Norman and we met at The Regency Tea Room close to Westminster Bridge the following day.

I found the tea room, without any difficulty it was newly built and had only opened a few weeks beforehand, it was bright and airy, and there were freshly cut flowers on each of the tables. I had arrived half an hour early, so I chose one of their homemade cakes, which they proudly advertised as having been baked using real eggs, and a cup of coffee. Norman arrived right on time, he greeted me with a peck on the cheek, making me blush once again. Our conversation was at first, awkward and stilted, but it didn't take either of us to relax. Before long we were chatting like old friends, or future lovers.

Norman told me all about his 6 years on the RAF prior to the war. He then went to America, where he studied to be an actor. He was successful and had several minor parts in films that I'd never heard of. I listened with fascination as he continued to tell me his story. He'd met his wife Celia, and they had a daughter, Margot, But Margot was born with a medical condition and his wife found it hard to cope. They returned to England just as the war broke out and Norman had to reenlist with the RAF.

Whilst Norman was away serving King and Country, Celia's mental state of health became worse; by the time the war was over, she had to be admitted into a specialised hospital, in the hope she would recover. Margot had been placed in the shared care of both grandparents and Norman. He told me about how difficult it had been for him having to leave Margot, to return to America to continue his acting career. He hoped that he would one day, gain custody of Margot and continue acting in England. He stopped at that point and looked at his watch.

'Do you realise that we have been talking for 2 hours?' He asked. I hadn't noticed. I could have listened to him forever.

We agreed to meet again the following week. But Norman rang me sounding rather distressed. He had just received a telegram from America, saying that he had been accepted for a part in a new film. He had to put his custody claim on hold and return with immediate effect back to the States. He would of course be in contact to let me know how things were going.

Selfishly, I was bitterly disappointed, I once again tore up his number, hoping that I would forget about him. I had even begun to believe that we could be more than friends. I didn't hear from him again for two years. During that time, I put all my energy into my dancing and even found time to start a relationship with a Russian male dancer.

When Norman rang me two years later, I was shocked and angry at his having to leave at short notice, and not keeping his promise to stay in touch. This was selfish of me, as I now realise. After a bit of persuasion, I agreed to meet him again, this time with Margot in tow. He explained that the film had taken longer than expected to make and Celia had given him a hard time with the divorce. He had finally gained custody of Margot and they now were living in a flat not too far from me.

I forgave him, and our friendship quickly developed into a relationship and then marriage. I eventually gave up dancing to devote myself to Margot's care. We later learnt that her condition was called 'Downs Syndrome', she was a loving, bright girl who also had a heart condition and died at the age of thirty-five. Norman continued acting until he retired, and we had a short but happy retirement. We went on cruises and saw places that I could only have dreamt about before I met him. It may have been a rough start for us together but we finished our lives together in style...

Soon after Norman passed away, I had a fall in the home Norman and I had shared for forty- seven years. Reluctantly, I agreed to become a patient at Pleasant View nursing home.

*

I must have fallen asleep again. Sarah was standing over me, at first, I thought she was cross.

'Mol, I expected you to at least be half ready, you've done nothing.'

'You promised to be back to help me in an hour' I retorted.

Sarah explained that she had been busy, with other clients and had forgotten the time. She looked at me closely, and apologised to me.

Sarah helped me get washed, I asked her to bring me a cardboard box from the wardrobe. Inside was the wedding dress. My mother made for me, from old bed linen and net curtains. It was yellower and more faded than I'd remembered. But it was still intact, and the moths hadn't eaten it.

'It's beautiful' Sarah said as she helped me put it on. Amazingly it still fit me.'

Soon afterwards Sarah announced the arrival of the television crew. She found me a wheelchair and we went down stairs in the lift to greet them.

The make-up artist came striding into the room unannounced, took one look at my face and said' 'Oh my God, never mind we'll soon have you looking fabulous darling'. It was then that I realised that I didn't have time to be bothered with make-up and looking fabulous. I really didn't have much time for anything at all.

I shooed him out of the room and told him that I'd rather be filmed without make-up; this didn't please him much and he stormed out of the room in a temper.

The rest of the party went by in a blur. The TV presenter asked my a few questions about my long stay at the home. Then both he and his crew departed. There was a huge spread for me and many of the past staff came to celebrate with me. I didn't eat anything; for some reason I wasn't hungry but after they had cut the massive birthday cake, and sang 'Happy Birthday' to me I said a final 'thank you' to all of them and asked Sarah to take me back upstairs. She helped me into bed.

I laid back on my pillows and closed my eyes. I heard Sarah's concerned voice talking to me, muffled at first, growing fainter, then nothing. Silence and darkness and a long tunnel, with a small light growing bigger and a tall, lean figure, with matinee idol looks waiting in that light; for me, yes, for me…

'I think it's time' I whispered, to whoever could hear.

*

Sarah looked down at Molly. *'A cantankerous woman at times, Molly',* she thought, but there was something about her that was endearing. Perhaps it was that she held an unshakeable love inside of her and which showed itself often enough to soften her moods and altered what others thought of her. Sarah felt that she would miss her after all these years. *'It was time'*, Molly had said. And it was true – she had waited long enough to be with Norman.

CAVING IN
By Janet Winson

Paralysed with fear, Amber thought she had suddenly gone blind.

Then she realised the torch had slipped out of her hand. She happened to be exploring a cave that morning as part of a group activity with some new friends and she was in real trouble now.

The torch had hit the ground with a thud and now she could hear it rolling, rolling away somewhere – and then the noise stopped. With a shiver, she realised there was nothing to stop it, no walls or furniture, nothing for it to roll under. And the blackness was total. No shape or volume, no clues to help her; nothing to tell her exactly where she was. She felt as if she had been captured by a giant black duvet that had been thrown over her head.

Terrified, but also angry with herself, Amber could not believe she had walked into this situation willingly. The build-up to the activity had caused her nightmares and she regretted that she hadn't listened to her inner voice and instinct, which had been telling her, screaming at her not to go.

Just entering the cave with the group had been a huge challenge and she wondered why she had continued but then recognised in herself her perhaps childish desire to go along with the crowd and, ultimately, make new friends. She imagined she may never see her two children again and thought of them playing at their grandparents' house with not a care in the world; guilt grew alongside her fear.

She had been following Fiona closely until the torch dropped; Fiona was always surrounded by her familiar floral perfume, which had calmed Amber until a few moments ago. Now, all Amber could smell was her own fear and the cave's dampness; there was no rose, patchouli or vanilla essence to mask it now.

"Help me!"

The cry hit the unseen walls but echoed into infinity. It had taken a lot of effort. She felt the panic grow inside her as she strained her ears for voices, murmurs but could hear nothing and see nothing – just the stifling darkness.

Amber leant against a cold, damp surface. Her heart was pounding; she hated her useless, trembling body, shivering equally with cold and fear. She felt her strength leave her as her knees locked and her thoughts became fuzzy, her brain slipping into a dreamlike state.

Suddenly, Amber thought she could taste soap and a very clear memory presented itself to her of an unhappy 12-year-old being dragged into the shower block at her boarding school by two girls who terrorised her regularly. A new girl without friends, who cried into her pillow most nights to stifle her misery. Everybody knew the nuns disappeared to the chapel as soon as the dismissal bell rang; there was no hope of a rescuer.

"Please stop, Marion. I'll give you all my sweet money. You can take my gold cross and chain and keep it!"

The two girls carried on relentlessly, pinching her and turning the cold tap on full so the freezing water ran down Amber's neck and soaked her blouse and skirt.

The memory started to fade, and the moment passed. She was back in real time once more, but Amber could still feel the wet droplets, which were now moisture from the cave walls.

She felt an arm around her, smelled a familiar waft of floral perfume. There was a round light shining in the space beside her. She was found – and the relief was immense.

"Silly sausage, we've been looking for you and now we've found you. Give me your hand." The recognition of Fiona's perfume and her comforting voice brought Amber back to her senses. Life was good.

FINDING ELLIE (A SCRIPT)
By Richie Stress

CAST:

GARY, 40s STEPHEN, 40s HANNAH, 13

GIRL, 13 ELOISE, 40s

STEPHEN
Look, I can't hold it much longer.

GARY
Look! Over there, in the far distance.

STEPHEN (studying carefully)
What, two old guys with walking sticks?

GARY
No, you idiot - the opposite direction. Behind you. It flew into the woods. Quick, follow me.

They arrive in the wooded area, both out of breath.

STEPHEN
I can't believe I agreed to come on another wild goose chase with you.

GARY (sotto)
Keep your voice down. You'll scare it off; and anyway, it's not a goose chase, it's a nightingale chase.

STEPHEN (sotto)
Well, whatever the hell it is we're in the middle of nowhere and I'm about to piss my trousers.

GARY (annoyed)
It's gone now - just go behind a tree or something and stop moaning.

STEPHEN
But what if someone comes?

GARY
Like who? There's nothing around here for miles. It's the ideal location for bird-spotting. Or it was.

STEPHEN
Yeah, but not ideal for my bladder. What about the old fellas we saw?

GARY
They were miles away and heading in the other direction. Just go already. I'll cough if I see someone.

STEPHEN
Ok, Ok.

SFX: AWKWARD RUSTLING THEN TRICKLING WATER. FAINT FOOTSTEPS APPROACHING FROM ANOTHER DIRECTION. A GIRL SINGING. GARY COUGHS.

STEPHEN (CONT'D)
Bloody hell!

SFX: SINGING GETS CLOSER. GARY COUGHS MORE LOUDLY. STEPHEN EMERGING FROM THE BRUSH.

HANNAH
Excuse me, my name's Hannah and I'm trying to find the old burnt-out house.

GARY
I don't think there's anything like that around here, Hannah. We passed an abandoned barn back there. You don't mean that?

HANNAH
No, I just came from there and a woman with a baby in a sling came to the door and told me it was this way.

STEPHEN
You sure you're in the right area?

HANNAH
I think so. I got a note from Ellie telling me to meet her at the old burnt-out house.

GARY
Well, if you carry on this way, then the path forks left and right, but beyond that I don't know, sorry.

HANNAH
Maybe I should try the right one then?

GARY
I guess it's worth a try.

HANNAH
OK, thanks anyway.

A BEAT.

STEPHEN
Look, if you can't find your friend than maybe you should think about heading home; before it gets dark.

HANNAH
I will. Nice to meet you.

GARY
Bye Hannah!

SFX: HANNAH WALKS AWAY SINGING TO HERSELF.

STEPHEN
Well, that was weird.

GARY
What? someone asking for directions?

STEPHEN
No. I mean the things she was saying about an old burnt- out house and the woman at the barn. That place was abandoned.

GARY
Maybe there's another barn somewhere.

STEPHEN
And, she was listening to a Walkman for god's sake, and the clothes she was wearing.

GARY
Yeah I did clock the Shakespeare's Sister t-shirt.

STEPHEN
Right! Who would wear one of those?

GARY
So, she's into the whole retro thing. It's no big deal Stephen.

STEPHEN
Yeah. I suppose. Look she's dropped something.

GARY
Must be the note from her friend, Ellie.

STEPHEN
Check it out, an embroidered handkerchief - 'E MORGAN' and there's an address. Maybe I should go after her.

GARY
No need.

STEPHEN
What do you mean?

GARY
Look the lights starting to fade and I've only had the briefest sighting of this bird. If there's an address, then we can just post the thing back to whoever can't we?

STEPHEN
Or you could take it round there yourself.

GARY
Ok, I'll drop it round tomorrow if that will make you happy?

STEPHEN
Cool.

GARY
You know the last recorded nightingale sighting was over 30 years ago.

STEPHEN
Jesus, you are such a geek

GARY
Are you coming or what?

STEPHEN
Yeah, wait up.

NEXT DAY. ELOISE'S HOUSE.

A girl answers the door.

GARY
Oh, hello, you must be Ellie?

GIRL
Hang on.
(Singing)
Muuuummmm.

A BEAT

ELOISE
Yes?

GARY
My name is Gary Springer. I think I found your daughter's
handkerchief and I wanted to return it.

ELOISE (shocked)
Where the hell did you get that from?

GARY
Your daughter's friend dropped it in the woods, but we didn't have
time to return it so I thought since this is her address then I should
bring it here.

ELOISE
What do you mean, you met my daughter's friend in the woods?
What friend?

GARY
Hannah. I assumed that's why she was meeting your daughter at the
burnt-out house to return it to her.

ELOISE
How do you know about that? No-one knows that.

GARY
Sorry, maybe there's been some sort of misunderstanding. I just
thought I should return the hanky to your daughter, *'ELLIE
MORGAN'*. That is her name right?

ELOISE
Mr. Springer, my name is Eloise Morgan and that handkerchief belongs to me.

GARY
But that's not possible?

ELOISE
You'd better come in.

INT. DAY. ELOISE'S HOUSE

FX: DOOR CLOSE.
FX: ELLIE STIRRING TEA

ELOISE
So, tell me what happened.

GARY
We'd just had this amazing sighting of a nightingale when I saw Hannah.

ELOISE
And then what?

GARY
She asked for directions to some old burnt-out house. I told her there were no houses around for miles, then she left.

ELOISE
But she'd dropped this handkerchief, correct?

GARY
Yeah, with your name and address on it.

ELOISE
This is gonna sound strange but Hannah was my best friend…she disappeared 30 years ago.

GARY
Wait a minute. So, you're saying the girl I met yesterday has been missing for the last 3 decades. But how?

ELOISE
You see I'd invited people to an abandoned house for my 13th birthday but Hannah never turned up.

GARY
So, what happened to her?

ELOISE
No one knows…but if what you're telling me is true there could still be a chance of finding out.

GARY
Oh my god – it just occurred to me. The nightingale I spotted; it was right before I met Hannah.

ELOISE
Sorry, I don't follow.

GARY
Well, I'm sure the previous sighting was in the same spot, 30 years ago- to the day. That can't be a coincidence surely…

ELOISE (sarcastic)
So, all we have to do is wait another 30 years and return to the same spot to find Hannah?!

GARY
Look I should be going.

ELOISE
You do believe me don't you?

GARY
Well, that handkerchief is real enough. Thanks for the tea, we should do it again some time.

ELOISE
Say in about 30 years.

GARY
It's a nice round number.

FADE OUT.

WHEN AM I?
By Richard Miller

My name is David, and you may have already heard this story. As with so many stories, it's good to hear or read them from someone else. It tells of my time serving with the United States Rangers in World War Two and what happened later; some would say a lot later. Hopefully things will become clearer – or possibly not. Most of this tale is set in 1944 but it's important to begin a couple of years before then.

As is well known, my country entered World War Two in 1941 after the Japanese attack on Pearl Harbor. There was some soul searching but I decided to join up; my decision was made easier by the fact that although my parents had emigrated to the US in the 1920s, they were born in Poland; Hitler's aggression against their home country was not something I could ignore. I joined the Infantry. Then, a few months later, I read about the newly formed Rangers and I knew that was for me.

In early 1943, I and others in my unit were sitting in our barracks when one of our sergeants marched in and shouted: "Right, you lot, in the next few days we're heading to the coast and then by ship to the UK. You'd best write to your nearest and dearest that you won't be seeing them for a while."

For some – and I hoped it didn't include me – that would mean not seeing our loved ones ever again. I would write to my parents and siblings but decided to phone them as well. Letters are nice but sometimes a phone call is a damned sight better. Off to one of the phone boxes in the barracks I went.

"Mama, it's David. I'm going to write you a letter but wanted to give you and Papa a call. It's finally happened; the boys and I are going to the UK. We've done a lot of training, but we want to do some proper fighting – especially those of us who have families in Europe and Britain." I had my grandparents and many aunts, uncles and cousins in Poland and hoped they were still alive. There were plenty of rumours about people being placed in concentration camps.

There was silence at the end of the line, and I could visualise my mother trying hard not to cry. "Mama, I know that me going off to fight is upsetting and I love you lots but I have to do my bit."

"I know, son… but your two brothers are wanting to join up. The thought of losing all three of you terrifies me and your father as well as your sisters. I shall be saying my prayers for you every day and going to Mass every Sunday."

"Thank you. And you never know, I might meet some lovely English girl, get married and give you a grandchild. If it's a girl, I'll name it after you and if a boy, after Papa."

"You know the way to my heart. Here's your papa for a word."

I heard my mother tell my father that I was on my way to the UK. "So, David, you're off to Britain. Give those Germans hell." I knew my father had a brother who had died serving with the Polish Army in 1939, so the war was very personal to him.

"I will do, Papa." As I said that, I knew he would be worrying as much as Mama and would attend Mass even though he wasn't as religious as she was.

"You take care, son. Your mama is now standing by the phone."

"Kocham was Mamo I Tato." For those of you who don't understand Polish, that means "I love you, Mum and Dad."

"Kocham, David."

I won't bore you with the details of the journey across the Atlantic but it's fair to say that there was always the fear of being sunk by a U-boat. The presence of US and Royal Navy ships was a comfort.

We landed in Northern Ireland and even though I spoke English, nothing prepared me for the accent that was spoken in that part of the UK. I really struggled to understand what was being said. It wouldn't be the first time I would struggle. Fortunately, there were some American soldiers who had been in Northern Ireland for some time and could translate for us.

Shortly after we arrived, a Rangers officer came over to us. His name was Colonel Watson and he was our commanding officer. He gave us his orders and told us what he expected of us.

"You'll be staying here for a few days and then we're off to Scotland for training with the British Commandoes. There's no need to tell you how good they are. Our top brass decided to form the Rangers to copy and learn from them. You are here to live up to those expectations. It will be tough, but you know the score. You should know that during the training live ammunition will be used. Yes, it will be frightening, but we need to be prepared and at the peak of fitness for when we invade Europe. The sergeant here will show you to your quarters."

A few days later, we arrived in Glasgow and, after a change of trains, headed north. On the train was a number of commandoes who would oversee our training. A few minutes before we were due to reach our final stop, a British sergeant major marched down the carriages, shouting. "Soon the train stops. We won't be met by trucks but instead you'll be marching in full kit to the camp. Only then will you eat. The march will be timed. Best to start as we intend to continue."

To say the next few weeks were tough would be an understatement. Lots of shelling, ducking under live bullets and, on the lighter side, learning a lot of new swear words and slang. We grumbled about the food but in our jobs we shouldn't expect fine dining. I learned that the British, despite what some of my fellow Americans think, are resilient bastards.

In July 1943, the order came through that we would be moving to the south of England for more training. It was obvious we were getting ready to invade Europe – but not when. We lowly troops just do what we're told. We ended up near Weymouth, in Dorset. A lovely part of the world. I have to say that, after the broad accents of Northern Ireland and Scotland, I found those in the south of England easier – though there was the odd occasion when I had to ask someone to repeat themselves. The locals would sometimes call us Yanks 'grockles'. It wasn't just Americans who were called grockles. Even those from other parts of Britain were; basically, they viewed us as outsiders or tourists.

It's important to know what happened next and who I met: someone who played an important part in my life.

When not training, we were allowed to visit nearby towns. One day, a few of us went to nearby Swanage, which is a lovely part of the world with some great pubs. It was at one of these – The Anchor – that I first glimpsed a lady who I can only describe as stunning. My comrades noticed the way I was looking at her.

"Go on, have a chat with her!" one said. "Ask her out. You never know, she might say yes."

I'd had a few girlfriends in the States and had been out a with a couple of women in Scotland, but this seemed different.

I wandered over to the lady. "Morning, ma'am. Do you mind if we have a chat?"

"Persuaded by your friends, were you?" She laughed. "I saw you looking at me. What will you do if I say no?"

"I'm sorry, I didn't mean to be rude." As I said that, her smile widened; it lit up her face and I knew I wanted to know her even more.

"Only teasing! It will be lovely to have a chat. After all, we've been told to be friendly to the colonials – especially as you're so far from home."

"Colonials?"

"You know. What we called you before you opted for independence." Again, another smile.

I gave her my hand, which she took in her own; it was small and soft. "My name is David. And yours?"

"Grace. After my nan." She looked at me steadily. "She's a lovely lady. If you behave yourself, I'll let you meet her."

"I'd like that very much."

The next few weeks were happy ones. Grace and I met as often as I was able to obtain time off and not only did I get to see her nan, but her parents too. They were a lovely family but I think we treasured those times when just the two of us would walk along those beaches that weren't sealed off, the waves beating alongside

It had to happen. As the months went by, it became obvious that we were getting ready to invade France. When and where in France was known to only a few on both sides of the Atlantic. Eisenhower was put in charge of the Allied Expeditionary Force, and we were confident that the top brass knew what they were doing – at least, it's what we hoped.

I had to decide whether to propose to Grace now or wait until the war was over. If she accepted, would it be fair knowing I could be shipped out at any time? In any event, I thought it right to let my parents know. A phone call to the States would have been the best way but use of them was forbidden and a telegram would be expensive; a good old-fashioned letter would suffice. Goodness knows how long it would take to arrive, if at all.

The letter went along the lines of this: 'Papa and Mama, I hope you are well. As I wrote a few weeks back, I've met a lovely English girl and I want to marry her. I've heard of men who have married and were then killed in action, and I don't really want to leave Grace a widow. At the same time, I love her dearly and don't know if I can wait until the war is over. I hope I have your blessing and it's a shame that you can't attend.'

The next day, I met Grace as planned and we went for a stroll along the beach. I stopped and got down on one knee. She gave me the courtesy of listening to my proposal. Then she smiled and said: "I wondered when you would ask me. The answer is yes."

I guess I shouldn't have been surprised that she knew I would ask her… I had made my feelings clear over the last few weeks.

The service was held in St. Mary's Church in Swanage and then we went back to The Anchor for some beers and a few sandwiches. Her parents, her brothers, and some of my Rangers comrades were present. Grace's brothers were in the Royal Navy and I would meet one of them again in different circumstances.

It was on April 20th, 1944 that I and my company were summoned to a briefing. At it, we were told we would be going on an exercise a week later in preparation for the invasion of Europe. From the 22nd, we would be confined to base; if we had family in England, we were advised to go and see them. Others would have to send letters or, if they could afford them, telegrams to the States.

As soon as the briefing was over, I borrowed a bike and cycled to Swanage. "Grace, I've got news for you."

I could see from her reaction that she had guessed what it might be: the news she had feared, that we were going to be parted and the very real danger that I would not return. But she merely nodded and replied, "So have I."

"You first." I hoped that on her side, at least, it was good news – and it was.

"I'm pregnant." I jumped up and down and gave my wife a big cuddle and a long kiss. "Now," she said, "tell me…"

I hesitated, then: "We're confined to barracks from the 22nd and going on exercise the 27th. I don't know the exact details, but it looks like we'll be invading Europe soon."

We had both known for a while that it would happen and that I would be involved, so we made full use of the next few hours. We walked, we talked and shed some tears before I finally returned to camp.

April 27th, 1944 is a date that will forever remain with me; it was the beginning of something I did not understand. Having headed to the coast near Slapton Sands, the company embarked onto naval landing craft. One of those craft was operated by Grace's brother, Alan. We formed an impressive flotilla, bobbing in the waves, white water moving us about, making it difficult to control the boats. In the distance, we could see ships of the US Navy. The plan was to practise landings on the beach in preparation for the big day – but then shouts began, quiet and puzzled at first, but swiftly changing into panicked screaming. It was then that I saw them.

German E-boats were in amongst us, firing, doling out death with their guns, the bullets zipping in and around us, until… My boat was hit. The torpedo heavily damaged the craft; that was something I could see even as I hit my head against a bulwark and ended up in the sea. The waters closed in above me, and then there was darkness…

*

"God, this water is cold!" was my first thought when I recovered consciousness. Then, as I gasped for air and felt a stabbing pain on the side of my head, I recalled the fire, the screams. I swam with panicked strokes as best I could towards the shore. But where were the other landing craft? Where was the noise? Where were my comrades? And the shoreline looked different to the one at Slapton Sands! Perhaps I'd drifted along the coast. There was something familiar about it though.

I swam with what strength I had to the beach. As I did, I thought: "Where is my rifle? That's my pay docked."

When I got closer to the shoreline, I noticed someone with binoculars looking out to sea; in fact, he was watching me. And when I staggered onto the beach, he rushed towards me.

"Hold on," he said.

I lay on my back until I was able to stand. I felt cold. "Where... where am I?"

"You're in Swanage Bay. Take it easy. Have you fallen overboard? Where's your boat?" He looked at me curiously, almost as if he had seen as a ghost.

"I was in Swanage a week ago and it didn't look like this. You're wearing jeans and a leather jacket. I haven't seen any Brits wear those." I noticed he was wearing a badge with 'Rolling Stones' on it. "Who or what are the Rolling Stones?" I asked.

"I often wear jeans and a leather jacket, and you must have heard of the Rolling Stones. A rock and roll band who also play the blues. They are big in the States."

"Well, I've sure heard of blues, but not rock and roll. These guys must be big in a different part of the States from me."

His next question rattled me. "I notice you're wearing a US Rangers uniform from World War Two. Are you part of a re-enactment? I'm not aware of anything going on."

That startled me because the British would have seen troops from the US Rangers. Made me a bit wary. And the way he said "from World War Two" as if it was a past event...

"Look, I'm not telling you anything more. You might be a bloody German spy." Bloody cheek asking me that question. As I stood there, shivering and confused, a strange-looking car drove past. It wasn't an automobile I knew but I recognised the badge. A Mercedes. "I can't believe you people would drive a car made by your enemy!" I said, astounded. "And talking of automobiles, where are all the military vehicles? There were loads weeks ago." I was now as confused as the person opposite.

"My name is Richard," he replied. "I'm interested in history – especially military – and that's why I recognised your uniform. Something's not right. If you're okay to walk, we can go to my place to get you dry clothes as you are cold and damp. You need drying off and perhaps to visit a doctor."

"History?" I was baffled, and gave him a quizzical look.

"I wouldn't be surprised if you don't believe me, but this is 2015 and the war ended seventy years ago. The Allies were victorious."

I felt weak, confused and was getting more and more angry. "You're right. I don't believe you. Just take me to someone in your or my army or the police. I'm cold and wet and not in the mood to be mucked about."

"Look, let's find a newsagent. I'll buy you a newspaper and show you the date. And then I'll take you to my place."

"So, it is 2015. January 2nd," I said, after seeing the newspaper. "What is £1.50? Whatever happened to pounds, shillings and pence? Last time I bought a paper, it only cost a few pennies!"

I was now very confused about where and when I was. My brain was hurting, not just from the confusion but also from the bang on the head when I hit the bulwark in the landing craft. If I was seventy years in the future, how come my head still hurt from the bang? Being in the future scared me and I couldn't help worrying about those I had served with – or should that be I am serving with?

Richard smiled. "Look, you're cold and wet. As I said, you can come to my place and put on some dry clothes. You look about the same size as me. It would be a better place to chat. I only live a few minutes from here and you can then ring the American Embassy, the police or whoever you want."

I was reluctant to go, but the thought of dry clothes and a call to the US Embassy swayed me. We arrived at his house and I was shown a room where I could change. Richard also told me where the bathroom was. The next few minutes gave me an opportunity to think about what to do and what to say to a total stranger who I still wasn't sure about. Speaking to the American Embassy would hopefully make things easier and clearer. I would find it better for my peace of mind to speak to a fellow American.

After changing, I walked into the lounge. There were many books, most of which were about past events. My host offered me something to eat and drink and let me settle. Then he rose and picked up one of the books; it was entitled *An Introduction to World War Two*. I glanced through it and it was some time before I could speak.

"Look, firstly, thank you for the clothes; I'm grateful. But none of this makes sense. I don't know who you are or what's going on but I'm going to ask you lots of questions and I want straight answers."

86

"I'm as confused as you are!" he said. "Hopefully from reading the paper and the book you are going to believe that it really is 2015. If you accept that, then you must also believe that anything I say is done with the benefit of hindsight – nothing I say is a secret – because it has already happened! I have two questions for you also: what is your name and exactly what date do you think it is?"

"Well, I'm willing to take a risk and trust you to an extent. My name is David. I'm not giving you my second name as I'm still sceptical about you. This may be an awful dream but for me, the date is April 27th, 1944." I paused and took another look at the paper. "So, we have a black president in the States. Barack Obama. Curious to know what he's like; Roosevelt is a hard act to follow. You say the war is over. I wonder how FDR celebrated?" I paused. "The last thing I remember was being in a landing craft approaching Slapton Sands. You know the area?" Richard nodded. "I was based in Weymouth and used to come along to Swanage on occasion. I met a lovely English girl, Grace. I married her not long after. Then, just before I had to be confined to base, she announced she was expecting. A boy or girl? Wonder where she is now. If she's still alive, she would be in her nineties. I suspect she re-married. I wouldn't blame her if she did. Maybe I could do some research. Anyway, why am I telling you about my family life? It has nothing to do with you."

I decided to talk only about my military experience. "I remember being in Lyme Bay, that's for sure. It was a German E-boat that fired upon our landing craft. A direct hit. I hit my head against a bulwark and ended up in the water. It's the last thing I remember. A bloody shambles. I wonder if the invasion was put back? I guess that was down to Ike, Monty and the others."

"Were you part of Operation Tiger?" asked Richard.

I looked at him; he obviously knew his stuff. "So, you know the name of the exercise. I guess it's no longer a secret!"

He smiled. "As I said earlier, I like studying military history. The invasion of France took place on 6th June 1944 and the Allies were finally victorious a year later." After a pause, my host – or could I call him my new friend? – continued. "After the invasion it wasn't all plain sailing, but the Germans surrendered in May 1945. Their allies, Japan, capitulated a few months later.

With the British, Canadians, Americans, as well as the French and Poles advancing from the west and the Soviets from the east, it was only a matter of time before the Germans surrendered. But they put up one hell of a fight, and thousands were killed, of course."

We talked. It was both fascinating and frightening. I was shocked to hear about Roosevelt's death. So sad. A great man. I was surprised the British people voted Churchill out of office given what he had done during the war. I thought they were ungrateful, but Richard said the country wanted a change. He also mentioned the difficult relations with the Soviets, which was not a big surprise as I felt the bond between us and them was strained; needs must at the time, I guess. The dropping of the two atomic bombs on Japan left me dumbstruck.

I was informed that Ike had served two terms as president in the fifties. Given that he commanded one of the biggest armies in history, that didn't come as a great surprise – he was a leader of men. Next, I was told about the landings on the moon. That was the biggest surprise of all. That silver globe so many miles away – men had set foot on it! As he talked, I felt that Richard was looking at me, testing to see if I was genuine. I can't say I blame him. My own story was as incredible as a human being landing on the moon. But if one can be true, why not the other?

Finally, I said, "I'd like to phone the US Embassy now, if that's okay."

Richard nodded. He pulled from his pocket a thin box, and said: "I'll call them now."

"God, is that a phone?! Where are the wires? Looks like a small radio."

He somehow looked up the number of the embassy on this phone and rang them. When someone answered, he passed the phone to me, and I started to speak. It was strange using this type of phone. I sensed this was going to be a difficult call and I wouldn't blame the people at the embassy if they thought I was a bit mad. In for a penny, in for a pound. An expression I'd learned during my time in Britain.

"Hello. My name is David Rejewski and I'm a member of the United States Rangers. My service number is 145903 and I joined up in 1942. The last thing I remember before ending up an hour or so ago in Swanage is falling overboard from a landing craft during Operation Tiger. I was helped from the sea by this guy, Richard. I'm in his house at the moment. You want to run some checks about my service? Makes sense. You probably think I'm mad. Not often you speak to someone who has lost the last seventy years. You want an address in Swanage and a phone number, and you'll call me back..." Richard wrote down the information and I gave the details to the person at the embassy. "You want to speak to Richard."

I handed the phone to Richard and he confirmed that he had helped me from the sea. I heard him say he would take a photograph of me and email it to them. What is email? He handed me the phone again.

"You're going to check my service records and then call me back and come and see me. It could be a few hours and you say the journey from London is three hours. Thank you." I returned the phone, and he hung up the call with the press of a button.

Richard looked at me carefully. "You said you were married to a lady called Grace. I heard you give your surname to the US Embassy. It's an unusual name. It's Polish, isn't it? I don't know how to put this, but I think your wife is my gran. Not many people with the name Grace Rejewski in Swanage."

I sat up with a start. "You mean she is still alive!"

"Yes." He nodded, slowly. "My grandmother has always lived in Swanage. My mum is her daughter. She has never spoken much about her time during the war. We always felt some tragedy had occurred that she did not want to talk about, although I think my mother knows a bit more than she's letting on. Gran brought up my mum by herself but her parents helped out when they could. They found it hard, as they lost my gran's brothers during the war. Both were in the Royal Navy. My mum's name is Sylwia..."

"How does she spell that?"

"S-y-l-w-i-a."

"The Polish way. Not the English. That's my mother's name." I'm not ashamed to admit that I cried when I heard that Grace had had to bring up our daughter by herself. But hearing that she had named our daughter after my mother filled me with pride and joy.

Mention of my mother made me realise that my parents would have long passed. Perhaps my siblings might still be alive, and if so, there was a good chance I may have lots of nephews and nieces as well as a daughter and grandson.

"Let me call my gran, and perhaps we can go and see her. We have some time before the people from the embassy arrive. We can also visit my mum and my sister. They live in the town as well."

I have a granddaughter as well.

Richard used that small, wireless phone again. "Gran, it's me. How are you? I have someone here who wishes to talk to you." He handed the phone to me, but before I could speak, he put his hand on my shoulder. "Be gentle," he whispered.

There was no need for him to say that. I know how to talk to people. My hand shook, and my voice with it. "Hello...Grace, it's David."

THAT'S PROGRESS, SWEETHEART
By Jan Brown

Rosemary Thomas, environmental activist, read through the latest threat to the local environment and ran her fingers through her curly hair. Another forest in danger of destruction, another campaign to mount.

She made the call. "Mum, are you ready for this one?"

*

The attack had been unexpected, brutal and relentless. Over 100 of us hacked down, crashing to an undignified end. Unable to move, I stood on the very edges of the horror, watching helplessly, trembling in the robust autumn breeze as the killing machines advanced towards me.

The morning had offered no clue of what was to come. As was normal, squirrels had chased rivals, burying and exhuming treasured nuts, and birds sang harmoniously, feathers fluffed and heads bobbed. All seemed well and safe for us, as it had for centuries. Then natural beauty was shockingly silenced by the terrifying roar of heavy machinery.

Some came to help us, with banners and barriers, shouting and protesting and horns to sound. We know we are loved by many, but some are blinded to beauty by the lure of profit and they came to destroy us with their harsh, unyielding hands and their unseeing eyes.

Quickly bound in heavy locked chains I was one of the lucky ones. Our branches temporary homes not to wildlife, for that had all fled, but to wildly angry people, old and young, desperate to join in the struggle to save us, for we are loved. When it finally ended the silence was absolute, no cheering but exhausted anger and sadness. I stood alone, isolated from my fellow survivors and surrounded by the slaughtered remains of my brethren, now mere shells piled high to be chopped and burnt. Their souls having already fled, they would weep no more. My branches drooped in sorrow.

Months later and the total silence that had descended on the forest after the attack was gradually being replaced by cautious tweeting and rustling. A stubborn morning chill had thrown a delicate sprinkling of frost over us survivors, but from a distance I could see the sunlit shafts rippling and dancing gently on new buds.

"Mummy", the little girl stood still, curly hair glistening in the weak sunlight. She looked across the deserted field, us survivors scattered wide. "Where have all the trees gone, and the birds; what's happened?"

Her tiny hand patted my knobbly bark and my leaves shivered with delight. I was bowed but not completely broken.

"That's progress sweetheart". Noting a quivering lip, she crouched down "but look Rosie, see the buds coming through and the little saplings. Spring always brings new life and will never give in."

They walked hand in hand.

"Of course, nature can always do with our protection and even a little assistance Rosie, maybe we can help somehow."

THE THIEF
By A.J.R. Kinchington

The dining room was a little noisy as Sylvia took her place beside her friend Mabel. 'Soup today, then chicken, and ice-cream for pudding. I like that and you do too, don't you, Sylvia?'

Sylvia nodded. She could not really say whether she liked it or not as it was difficult sometimes to remember the taste of certain foods.

Kathy the helper served their meals and afterwards escorted the two ladies to the TV lounge. It was two o'clock but it was becoming gloomy outside and Sylvia thought: *Gloomy in this vast lounge. Sunny Dale Care Home seems at odds with the weather.*

They both crossed the room and looked out at the large garden, where a small boy was chasing the birds off the lawn. Two other children ran around and their obvious pleasure and freedom had the two friends smiling.

'Free,' Sylvia said, softly. Kathy came over to the two friends and motioned them to their chairs.

Agitated and angry, Sylvia suddenly shouted at the room: 'I've been robbed, robbed!'

'Let's sit down and talk this through,' said Kathy, once again trying to steer the two companions to the seats.

'Did you not hear me? I have been cheated, robbed,' Sylvia said, defiantly.

'No one has robbed you,' said Kathy, gently.

'Oh, yes, yes they have!' Sylvia said, now allowing herself to be guided to her chair. Mabel said nothing but sat holding Sylvia's hand.

Kathy went to the Welfare Officer's room, where Jamie was occupied on his computer. 'We are having problems with Sylvia again. She insists she has been robbed but there is nothing missing from her room or belongings. What should I do?'

Jamie was new to the job, fresh from his short psychology course and eager to make a good impression on the Care Trust. 'We can talk to her in the morning. Her 99th birthday tomorrow may cheer her up. She has probably got disturbing memories. I will assess her tomorrow.' He returned to his computer, which told Kathy the conversation was over. She had known Sylvia for the last five months and knew this dignified lady was not one to be taken lightly.

The following morning, Jamie gathered his papers and headed towards Sylvia's room, collecting Kathy on his way.

Her room was neat and tidy. Hairbrush and lipstick evenly placed on her dresser. The mirror above *'told lies'*. The silver locket was polished, ready to wear, and Sylvia fancied her small, pearl earrings would be perfect. She knew today was her birthday – a big one, so everyone said – but she had always counted every birthday as a celebration. There was to be a party later with family and friends. She smiled at the thought.

Kathy knocked and entered, followed by Jamie. 'Morning, birthday girl,' said Jamie.

Sylvia nodded. *How patronising. Girl indeed. I am all the woman I expected to be at 99 years old.*

'Shall we have a chat?' said Jamie, sitting on the edge of her bed. 'I hear that you think you have been robbed. Why would you say that?'

'Because I have.'

'What do you believe has been taken?'

'Why are you asking me? There is nothing you can do.'

'Let me see if I can. Are you having nightmares of times past? Seeing things, hearing things that disturb you?'

'No.'

Sylvia stared at him, until finally he said: 'Perhaps we can have another chat again.'

Not if I can help it.

Jamie rose and she smoothed out her quilt.

He took his notes and wrote, *Suffering from PTSD. Age related. Research.*

*

The day went ahead with the party. Sylvia was told that it was from twelve o'clock until two p.m.

I remember when parties started at two p.m. and finished at two a.m. That would be more like it. Still, must not grumble.

She gratefully accepted her cards and gifts and was happy to see her daughter, grandchildren and great grandchildren.

'Grannie, what is it like to be nearly a hundred?' asked Tracy, the youngest of the children, who, at eleven years old, was the livewire of the group.

'When I was your age, I remember taking my dad's hand as we walked to London Bridge. As a teenager, I danced all night and rode pillion on my boyfriend's motorbike. I'm the mother of your grannie, so the old lady you see today is because of all these times.'

'Are you sad that all these times are gone?'

'No, not at all.' *I have so much more I could tell you.*

Tracy seemed content with her answer.

After the family left, Jamie came to see her. 'May we have another talk, Sylvia? I think I can help you. There is a such a condition as PTSD. That is, Post Traumatic Stress Disorder – and we can help you to process that and help you to be less anxious.'

What the hell is this? He doesn't have a clue. 'Disorder? I do not have a disorder. I tell you again, I've been robbed. We all were.'

'Who is we, and what has been stolen?'

Sylvia snorted and took a deep breath. Her eyes seemed to send out sparks. Her voice was strong and steady. 'All of us that lived through the war. Time was stolen. TIME. Time to live without fear, to love, to plan, just knowing we were free of heartache and losing loved ones.' She rose from her chair, paced the floor and seemed to grow in stature. It was as if the years disappeared and she was a vibrant woman once more, full of emotion and fire.

Jamie and Kathy were perplexed by how to respond to this woman so full of passion and anger.

Sylvia spat out: 'War is the thief, robbing everyone then and everyone now. Look at the people of Ukraine and Russia. I watch the thief and despair.' She was spent now and politely addressed Jamie and Kathy. 'I'm going to my room. Perhaps you will believe me when I say I've been robbed and there is nothing you can do to fix it, but I thank you for your concern.'

With that, she walked with an air of dignity to her own small space.

Later, Jamie and Kathy made an adjustment to their notes and agreed that indeed she had been robbed.

*

Mabel knocked on her door, came in and sat beside her friend.

'I've explained to them what I mean, but not the whole story,' Sylvia said.

'Do you want to tell me?'

'I was robbed of the moments, those few moments when I could have told Ted that I was pregnant. Our wedding was planned for two days later. He was killed before we had the chance to live. We met at a dance that had been planned for the service men and women. He was American, in his twenties; tall, blond, not that handsome – but he had the most beautiful smile. He was coming home but an air raid bombed the library building and he was caught up trying to rescue people. He was hit by falling masonry and died instantly. We had been so trusting in our future together. War, the time thief; we never get that time back.'

'Sylvia, would you really want to go back to that awful time?'

'Oh, in a heartbeat. Being with Ted for one more moment is all I would have needed.'

'When you married Bert, did he know about Ted?'

'Yes, and my precious girl, Teresa. She has her father's blue eyes and special smile. Bert treated her like his own.'

'You still get angry, Sylvia.'

'Those who don't rage against wars, those who witness the injustice of it, might as well be dead themselves.'

The two friends sat in silence, each with their thoughts.

LONG GONE SILVER
By Tony Ormerod

Don Silver could no longer contain his anger or moderate his language.

'Bloody hell, bloody hell. Come on!'

No matter; no one was listening. He was alone, driving his car and stuck at yet another red light. Beating the steering wheel with both hands, he wondered why there were so many roadworks and so little evidence of workmen.

'It's bad news, darling,' he rehearsed out loud. That would probably be his immediate reply when he opened the door of the house and his lovely wife would, with some excitement, some expectation, enquire if, following the interview, he had got the job. At last, the green light glowed brightly, inviting him to proceed. He began to think back over the details of a dreadful afternoon.

True, his new boss, initially, surprisingly, and appearing to be very kind, had congratulated him on forty years of loyal service to the company and, latterly, thanked Don for his support at a difficult time. Everything then went downhill. He had expected a sizeable panel to be sitting in judgment, considering the importance of the vacancy, not to mention a significant hike in his income. Instead, the boss, to Don's embarrassment, had merely enlisted the support of his latest conquest, Gloria, the Human Resources Officer.

Young, blonde, Don knew her well and felt her presence was inappropriate. In fact, it was unprecedented. Undoubtedly, she was attractive and intelligent – but his late mother, he thought, would have described her as "a madam". Human Resources! Whatever happened to Personnel? It soon became clear that the lovely Gloria had been tasked with overseeing the coup de gras to his long, distinguished career. She too paid him a couple of compliments before getting down to business. Clearly, it was not a job interview.

There followed a short monologue. Words like 'downsizing', 'new challenges', 'new blood', 'new technology' and, inevitably, the long-term effects of Covid served to lead to an inevitable conclusion: redundancy. Oddly, he thought, there was an admirable efficiency about her, but then he supposed he had always known that. He *was* 58 years old.

Every few seconds, he glanced towards the much younger man who had recently inherited the firm following the sad death of his father, Joe Barnes, the founder of the company and Don's closest friend. James Barnes was not like his late father: not in favour of *Auld Lang Syne* or employees past their usefulness, as he had told Don on more than one occasion, hammering home that point frequently by stressing the need to accept all the new technical methods of working more productively. James regarded the older man as someone who was content to remain rooted in the past; a dinosaur who simply could not or would not accept that the business world had changed. But James could relax now. Gloria had been supplied with the bullets and seemed content to fire the gun.

'So that's that then?' Don had stood and glared down at the two of them. Speaking softly but with feeling, he'd added, 'Gutless as usual, Jim lad. Leaving the dirty work to your bit of fluff?'

In contrast, the boss, furious, had leapt to his feet, shouting: 'Don't call me Jim; it's sir to you – and just keep your big mouth shut!'

'Call you sir? No, no chance, mate. You are not half the man your dad was. Anything else – or are we done here? I'll go quietly. Using her for this?' He'd leant towards his boss, who shrank back into his chair a little. 'You should be ashamed and you deserve a bloody good hiding!'

As he'd turned to leave, he'd halted when Gloria spoke. 'Excuse me. I think you might be interested in this.' She had held out an envelope. Later, he regretted the childish way in which he had rudely snatched it from her grasp. Unfazed, she'd tidied her notes as she'd added: 'Let's face it, you have not moved with the times!'

He had not been sure but, with hindsight, had she winked then?

Usually, it took about an hour for Don to drive home from his office, but tonight he was dawdling. A glance at the dashboard clock confirmed that. It was no surprise, considering he had been deep in thought and not in a hurry to arrive. What would his wife Maureen say about his new situation? She, who had supported him through good times and not so good; she, who had spent many hours bringing up two children on her own when he was working long hours; she, who in earlier days had contributed so much financially to making a fine home for the two of them.

Suddenly, he felt very tired. He had just passed a road sign meant for those who travelled much longer distances, reminding them that tiredness could kill and urging them to take a break. Deciding to take that sensible advice himself, he looked for, then quickly found, a side road. On turning into it without signalling, he was mildly annoyed when the driver of the car following close behind expressed his feelings with a loud, drawn-out use of the horn.

'Tough Cheddar!'

There were no yellow lines in the well-lit road and plenty of room for his car, so he pulled up not far from the main road and sat back in his seat. After toying with the idea of using his mobile to telephone his wife, he realised she would enquire about the interview. No, it was not a good idea. That could wait. And anyway, she was used to him coming home late.

For the first time, he thought about his future. Stacking shelves at Sainsbury's or similar did not appeal and he had felt sorry for the British Airways pilot who, thanks to Covid, had settled for delivering groceries by van. Damn! He had been so vexed, so in a hurry to get out of the bloody interview that he had not mentioned money. Compensation, settlement, whatever it was called.

Closing his eyes was the priority, so he used the wheel built into the seat to convert it to the recline position and settled back. At first resisting the urge to sleep, he succeeded for a while. Then, trying hard to put his disappointment behind him, he smiled to himself when he recalled the number of people who, over the years, had asked him if he was related to his namesake, Long John Silver. An uncle, something of a comedian, had, with tall tales of derring-do, convinced him that he, Don and the infamous pirate were related. When he was nine, an older brother, aged eleven, had been delighted to shatter his illusions at about the same time that he told a tearful younger brother that Santa would not be calling round.

He permitted himself another slight, sad smile at those long-ago memories and then felt himself drifting, drifting into sleep. Finally, fighting against it, he surrendered into the arms of Morpheus. He was not a prodigious dreamer but...

*

Long Don Silver had come a long way from humble beginnings. A callow youth, he had been lured from the comfort of his Cornish home with the promise of untold wealth and adventure on the high seas. On his first ship, as a lowly cabin boy, thrown overboard as bait by a vicious crew, he was cruelly savaged by a shark. Minus his right leg but, thankfully, alive, he turned his hand to cooking and found himself catering for the even worse crew of a pirate ship; there was criticism. One day, encumbered by his disability, he was attacked by a dissatisfied drunken vegetarian who gouged out his left eye with his bare hands. A black eye patch, a custom-made wooden leg, an untended beard, plundered ill-fitting clothes and an incontinent talkative parrot who never left his right shoulder gave him a frightening, intimidating aspect; handy advantages in the pirate fraternity.

Now a much-changed man, a captain at the pinnacle of a career that had finally brought himself and his ship to an anchorage off Hispaniola, there was unease about some of the changes, which were slowly eating away at his very soul. His crew, a sullen, ragtag bunch of malcontents, had grouped themselves untidily amidships around the main mast when a weary Long Don emerged from his cabin to issue his commands. Some smoked, some chewed and spat out tobacco, others, against orders, continued to drink grog, and the all-pervading stench of fifty men who were unenthusiastic about personal hygiene drifted towards him. There was also the unmistakable whiff of mutiny in the air.

'Let's get to 'em, shipmates, there be plunder for us all on yonder shore!' cried the gallant captain as he hobbled gamely to the port side and raised his cutlass in the general direction of the land.

'Careful now with that, Cap'n, you'll be having someone's eye out!'

Long Don rolled his own eye in frustration. He was beginning to wish he'd never left England. His wooden leg was riddled with dry rot and his crutch had seen better days, but no repairs were available since the alcoholic ship's surgeon had provided a questionable long-term sick note for his drinking chum, the carpenter. In spite of that, just when the old campaigner was at last beginning to get into something resembling his stride, that officious below-deck lawyer was bleating on at him again.

'Jim lad, what's the matter now, blast you?' Long Don, clearly irritated, turned towards the man, almost falling over, but managed to regain his balance by skillful use of his crutch.

'I have a job to do, you know, Cap'n, and it's more than it's worth to let you swish your thingy about without due care and attention.'

The veteran buccaneer was about to deliver one of his famous broadsides but, with a superhuman effort, he held his tongue, reminding himself that the man had been foisted on him by the recently formed Pirates Confederation. In the distant past, the pipsqueak – something to do with "safety" – would have been keel hauled but now... well, that particular aid to maintaining good discipline, together with 'walking the plank', had been grudgingly withdrawn.

Silver shrugged his shoulders and turned his attention to more important matters. 'Man the longboats, mateys!' He continued to brandish his cutlass in defiance.

Someone was tugging at his coat. 'Excuse me, Captain.'

'What now?' He looked down at the effeminate, slightly built sailor who until now he had noticed but studiously ignored.

'Did you mean 'person the longboats', Captain?'

'Shiver me timbers. You sound like a woman!'

'I am a woman, Captain. The name's Gloria.'

Long Don Silver shook his massive head in disbelief, just managing to hold onto his best – albeit a size or so too small – tricorn hat before it tumbled to the deck. Here was yet another example of those who were undermining his authority. How he yearned for the good old days.

After inching his way down a rope ladder with some difficulty, he clambered clumsily into one of the boats. Then, standing at the prow, he prepared to bark out further orders.

Captain Flint spread elegant wings, emptied his bladder onto his master's shoulder and lifted his little feathered head. 'Health and safety, equal opportunities!' he squawked.

It was the final insult. His best friend had turned on him. 'What happened to 'pieces of eight', you traitor?' An incensed Long Don seized the poor bird, viciously twisted its neck and hurled the lifeless body into the sea in one continuous movement.

There was a short pause.

One of the hands downed his oars, took out a small, well-used, grimy notebook from a long coat of uncertain age and, after rooting around in a pocket, withdrew a tiny pencil which he licked energetically, before fixing his captain with an icy stare. 'In my capacity as ship's representative of the PPL, I must report this incident, Cap'n. Full name, if you please.'

'PPL? What's the PPL? Damn your eyes – and how dare you talk to me like that!'

'The Parrot Protection League, of course.'

The crutch, thrown with some force, narrowly missed the rep's head and fell harmlessly into the sea. With a muttered oath the old sea dog, Long Don Silver, leant over and, with a huge sigh, gradually allowed himself to slide into the blue waters of the Caribbean Sea. Within seconds, he was gone. A wooden leg and a crutch bobbed to the surface, the signal for spontaneous applause from a couple of the hands who, loyal to the end, had witnessed their captain's demise.

'A brave and fitting conclusion to a great career,' murmured oarswoman Gloria. 'Sadly, he just couldn't move with the times!'

*

Don's car seat had proved comfortable enough when he had fallen asleep, but when he suddenly awoke, arms and legs thrashing about all over the front seats of the car, his every limb, neck and back seemed to be aching. Drenched with sweat, he reflected that it was rare for him to remember dreams but that one had seemed real. Dreaming of himself drowning in his car? It was silly, comical, impossible, but a bit frightening. Switching on the interior light and then reaching over to the passenger seat for his jacket, he produced a packet of wet wipes from the inside pocket. He stepped outside and circled the vehicle for a few minutes, stretching his legs whilst dabbing away at his face before, shivering now in the night air, he returned to the warmth of the car. It was 5pm. He had promised Maureen he would phone as soon as he left his so-called interview, but the bad news could wait.

It was then, as he deposited his jacket on the passenger seat, that he spotted the forgotten envelope. Ripping it open, he briefly scanned its contents. He could not believe his eyes. Out loud, incredulous, muttering an oath, he exclaimed: 'No, that's ridiculous, that's impossible!'

Starting the car, anxious to reach home, he exceeded the speed limit more than once.

*

Maureen Silver had spent most of her day mooching around the house. As was usual with her husband, he had left early for his office after consuming a substantial breakfast, hurriedly kissing her on the cheek as he rushed out, leaving her nibbling nervously on a piece of toast. She just had time to wish him 'Good luck for this afternoon!' before the front door slammed. Her husband had been confident that the job would be his; surely the interview was a mere formality?

Less sure, she had her doubts. Facing him, talking to him, she had pretended to share his optimism, feigned excitement at the prospect of extra income. Never someone who could be described as pessimistic, she was enough of a realist to know when things could go awry. Don had mentioned on several occasions that he and the new owner of the company did not see eye to eye. That fact alone would count against him if, as was normal, the interview panel was headed up by James Barnes. The man was a serial adulterer; she loathed him.

Don and Maureen had met and married after the proverbial whirlwind courtship. Their son had emigrated to Australia in his twenties, prospered over there and married an Australian girl who they had only met twice when they returned on holiday to England. However, they were both happy for their son and daughter-in-law.

Their daughter, a few years older, intelligent, strong-willed, ambitious and attractive, had graduated with honours at Oxford. Unfortunately, she had left home after a silly argument and carved out her own career. Maureen had heard rumours, since confirmed, that she had taken up with a married man and had been set up by him in a paid-for apartment. It was the last straw as far as her mother was concerned. Adamant in her refusal to consider the girl still her daughter, Don's pleas that she should accept or at least tolerate the situation were not successful. It was their only serious disagreement in close on 35 years, but one which had sorely tested their relationship.

Maureen consulted the clock on the kitchen wall. It was after five o'clock in the afternoon and still there was no word from Don. He had promised, win, lose or draw as he had put it, that he would contact her as soon as he had been interviewed, but apart from one call from a double- glazing firm, the phone had remained silent.

'No news is good news,' she told herself, with little confidence, as she absent-mindedly sipped at a stone-cold cup of tea. It was a tiny crumb of comfort on an afternoon of rising gloom and doom. Stealing a glance at the expensive brand of champagne nestling in an ice bucket, her mind was made up. If the company big noise failed to recognise all the long, hard, extra unpaid hours her husband had spent working for both him and his father, and a deserved promotion was denied to Don, so be it. The bottle's contents would be consumed and enjoyed, win, lose or draw.

The flash of headlights and the sound of a car driving up the sideway before pulling up in front of the garage sent her hurrying to the front room, where she parted the curtains and peered out into the darkness. It always amused Don. 'Why? Were you expecting one of your boyfriends?' was his usual question, but there were variations. His face, she noted, as he entered the house, betrayed nothing.

'Well, sweetheart, how did it go?' She asked the question excitedly but feared the worst.

'Do you want the good news or the bad news?' Don said, as he casually leant over to the small table that held the champagne and freed it from its ice cooler. There was a pause, allowing him to deftly remove the foil from the bottle and then begin the task of untwisting the metal wiring holding back the cork. 'Well, go on then. What do you want first – good or bad news? I'm waiting.'

'Oh, I don't know. Must we play that silly game?' Maureen hesitated for a few seconds before finally surrendering. 'Okay, the bad news first, please.'

'I've been sacked!' The cork shot out of the bottle before hitting the ceiling and landing behind a sofa. It signalled a gasp, followed by floods of tears from Maureen; the creamy-coloured liquid seemed to follow suit as it streamed out onto her new carpet.

'That's not fair! All you've done for that bloody firm,' she sobbed. 'That bastard Barnes, was it?'

Don nodded and busied himself pouring expensive fizz into one of the two glasses provided, before any more could be wasted on the carpet. He offered the drink to his wife and she reluctantly accepted it. Wiping away some tears with the back of her hand, she sniffed and enquired of the 'good news'.

'Have a read of that letter, love.' He pointed to the envelope, which he had placed next to the ice bucket on arrival. 'I think you might be pleasantly surprised.' Maureen raised her glass to her mouth but before she could sample the contents, Don intervened. 'Not now, darling. Wait for the toast.'

Puzzled, she did as instructed. Putting down her glass, she picked up the envelope and removed its contents. It was a single, typed sheet of company notepaper. Her eyes widened as she struggled to come to terms with the contents. An extremely generous early retirement, index linked pension and an enormous cash sum in recognition of her husband's excellent service over many years were mentioned. But it was the signature and the handwritten message at the foot of the letter that brought

Maureen to tears again. 'PS,' it read. 'Mum, Dad, I still love you xx'

'How did it happen? How could it be?' Maureen mumbled. 'Not now, love. A bit later, eh? Come on, Maureen, let bygones be bygones.' Don raised his glass and motioned his still sobbing wife to follow his example. 'To Gloria Silver, our clever girl!'

A LITTLE TIME OF CHANGE
By Janet Winson

I think I may have mixed my drinks, one night last week. I woke up feeling perfectly normal, yet within minutes found that things weren't inclined to stay that way. Not at all.

When I sauntered towards the mirror and ran the hairbrush across my head I was expecting to see and feel the same thick, long hair – greying, I know – that I'd had for years. Instead, I yelled in pain as the bristles scratched my scalp. Frowning, I got up close to the mirror and focused on my reflection. I can tell you; I didn't like what I saw – I had no hair on the crown of my head!

The rest looked familiar, alright – it was a face I recognised, but not my own. The eyebrows and eyes were mine, though seemed darker than usual. Then it hit me, and I gasped. "Oh God…"

I was looking at Jim, my eldest son.

I began to sweat, and asked myself what the hell was going on – not an unreasonable question. Then it struck me. "Blow me down, I've morphed into my own son!"

I thought back. I had got out of bed easily with no aches or pains, no need for any painkillers for my knees – for once. I had a sudden change of outlook and said to myself, "Well then, today is the day to get the hoovering done and sort out the pile of junk in the loft. Oh yes, today I am strong and fit as a fiddle!"

But it didn't work out like that.

In the kitchen I fed the cat, as was my routine; he seemed to like me more than usual, purring and rubbing himself around my extremely hairy legs. I was horrified at the thought of them – but I went along with everything. I had no choice – and there was a lot to do.

The Fruit and Fibre didn't make it to the bowl. I was searching for something different to eat. I counted the eggs in the fridge and, in moments, I was frying the most enormous breakfast ever. It covered the biggest plate in the rack and the beans were falling over the sides of the plate. I knew damn well this was far too much food and full of fats and carbohydrates, but

I couldn't help myself. Soon, I was taking a photo of the big breakfast and posting it to Facebook.

The food went down a real treat with two big cups of tea. Whilst eating, I realised that at some point I had switched Alexa over to XFM from my usual Classic. I normally hated XFM and had spent the past 20 years switching it off!

Instead of sorting washing and emptying the dishwasher I was suddenly climbing the stairs two at a time, into the back bedroom and onto the dusty old exercise bike, which I was constantly on the verge of chucking out. I did a good, fast 30 minutes on it as the sweat ran down my new body. I had my reservations but thought these good knees were worth keeping; I wasn't so keen on the rest though.

In a nutshell, none of the heavy housework got done and, after an overlong shower and plenty of Lynx, I sat downstairs with the remote, channel-hopping until I found a documentary dedicated to *Secret Files on Alien Landings in the USA*. There I sat, remote at the ready, custard creams in the biscuit tin and a supersize mug of hot chocolate. Within two minutes I was immersed in the programme – and time passed…

Suddenly, the phone rang. Groggily, I wondered who it was. I picked it up.

"Hi Mum, are you at home all day today?"

Hang on, this was Jim calling! I counted my blessings that he had his own voice, not mine. I looked down at myself – the legs were no longer hairy.

When he rang off, I tipped the vodka down the sink. I'm on the wagon for the foreseeable now.

THE SPECTRE OF DEARG
By C.G. Harris

I struck out for Glen Dearg in such condition as one should always be when taking a full day's hike – namely, fully rested from a night on eiderdown, fortified by a farmhouse breakfast and bidden farewell with a smile from the landlady's daughter. Of whom I will speak more – the landlady, not the daughter – after you have heard such grim and bloody goings-on as I shall describe; for, being a Highland farmer's wife, she was doubtless aware of the Spectre of Dearg yet told me not a jot before I set off.

There may be those fresh from St. Andrew's who consider themselves a cut above those without such an education – but I, though a scholar of the class of 1887, was not of that ilk. In honesty, what did I know of crofting, of sheep or cattle or farming or the tilling of land, and hardships endured? My travels found me close to those who faced such things, and faced them with fortitude; they were hospitable and viewed the preparations for my daily walks with a smile and a raised brow, for the most part leaving me to it but at other times offering all manner of advice. I was wise enough to take it.

Therefore, I set off leather-booted, warm-socked and trousered, waterproofed in jacket and with a backpack full of such essentials as had been advised. Was there forewarning of what was to come? An encounter born of redress and sacrifice and a bond transcending time – you may call it love if you wish, for I so do. Did I feel it as, setting out, a mist rolled across the heather in waves and a wind whipped about me, angry and chill? Perhaps for a moment I paused…but then stepped forth with the gusto of youth and took the first stile almost with a bound. The glens and hills faced me several miles distant and the sun rose, though with little warmth, and somehow burned away the mist.

My thought was to traverse this high moorland north for three or more hours, drink tea and eat beside a thin loch they called Rutthers. Thereafter, I would head upwards and across whale-back hills and down into Glen Dearg – I was told the scenery was worth the labour – making my way to the once market village of Gillen a few more miles from a small loch at its farther end; there I would find lodging for the night and return the next day.

I had no need to break trail. I followed an old drovers' path and, as the morning wore on, I began to feel the weight of historic footfall upon it and upon myself. It was that of human and animal, cattle being driven to market as they had once been for generations gone by; it tied me to both past and present at a time and I found that this led me to a melancholic mood – the skies, now overcast, assisted in moving me to this. So, I bowed my head against the wind and determined to make Rutthers swiftly; refreshment in shelter, could I but find any, might raise my spirits. When I finally gained that loch I found a douce surprise – a compound of stables used by drovers as a final respite before they pushed on up and over into Glen Dearg. I huddled inside and sipped and supped on tea and nuts and cake. I watched waves whip up across the loch, and listened to the wind whoop and hiss as it snaked in and out and around the structures, still sturdy despite cracks and splinters in the wood.

It was as I stood and stretched and raised my eyes to gauge the steepness of the hills to come that I saw him: a figure, a fellow hiker, difficult to define in character and size at such a distance and in this light. He was pushing up strongly amongst the crags towards the plateaued brow where the yellow- green moor grass turned purple-brown, the glen beyond for centuries past thereby being assigned the term Dearg, meaning red, though it was not so in the truest sense. In a moment he was gone – at the zenith a dark shape laid bare against a weak, cloud-covered late autumn light – and curious though I was to find another like myself alone amongst this wild and wind-strafed landscape, I thought of it little more but made comfortable the pack on my back, then sighed and puffed in concert with the wind as I followed upwards the path that he had taken.

It was an hour and more before I reached the peak – an hour of straining sinew – but what a glorious vista lay below! The aforementioned heather covered slope after slope, almost burgundy it seemed to me, and rivulets wound between it, down and down to a valley where the grasses were green and a stream ran along more swiftly than I would have imagined towards the loch, tawny in the distance.

Of the stranger, I saw no sign – until of a sudden, after a half mile of descent, with a few craggy boulders on either side, I felt a presence at my shoulder and a voice at my ear. More a statement than question, but pleasant enough: "You'll be heading for Gillen as well, then?"

Surprised, I turned sharp and saw a young man of middling height and build like myself. He was as sensibly wrapped as I but I would hazard to say he was tougher than me beneath the layers, for below his hair, which was fair and tousled, his blue eyes were steady, though watering in the wind, and he had the steadfast jaw of a teuchter, one who lived in wild country and determined never to complain of it.

"Och man, you fair startled me," I said.

I was a little on the put-out side until he nodded and smiled and said: "If you dinna mind the comp'ny, I'll be alongside you the way."

He then strode a little ahead and I found myself calling after him, "I'll welcome it, thank you...!" and quickening to keep pace.

Now...if you are of the doubting kind, a scoffer at the bar, a roller of the eyes and a shaker of the head, turn down this page and read no more. Desist to read, I tell you, for I relate to those with minds and hearts as open as my own; though they once were not.

But should you pursue...well...you may sometime find yourself at fireside, alone, with glass in hand, rain at window and a wind beneath the eaves; there may be darkness without and a glow within and the logs may crackle with the spirit of it all; and you will recall hereafter that which I have to say of Jamie Campbell.

Aye, Jamie...for that is how he introduced himself and I returned with a name of my own: Alastair.

He replied with but a nod and set a pace that gave little opportunity for idle chat until we descended to the aforementioned stream. We followed alongside, with only its burblings to break the silence until I ventured a few remarks.

"You'll be from these parts, I'd say?"

"Aye, can you tell?" he replied.

"Well now, you swing along as if you know the place. Your tread is steady and sure."

He smiled, a little sadly, I thought. "Aye, I've trod this path more often than most." He gazed ahead, then at the peaks of the hills on either side; I noticed, for the first time, rain-filled clouds, billowing and black. "Aye," he said, softly, "for far longer than I've wished," although this made no sense to me at the time.

Crossing the stream at a little ford, we stepped in single file from pale granite rock to rock. As we did, I glanced at Jamie's back and started. He had no pack! And yet...I'll swear by all that's holy it was there upon our descent. Frowning, I shouted from behind: "Och, man, where's your pack?!"

"Pack?" He shrugged. "I have no need. I have my bedroll and sporran." He faced me and these said items hung loosely in front. In his hiking gear they were out of place, but he adjusted a strap, swung the bed roll across his shoulder and to his side and continued.

I floundered like a salmon and splashed out after him. "But where have they co-?"

"Tchh, we have a way to go, Alastair, if you are to be safe."

"Safe?"

But he was away striding...striding, and the clouds gathered close and dark, packed with rain. Light droplets began, sheeting in the wind.

"Man, wait for me!" I cried.

Within a minute I had gained upon him and reached his shoulder. Which I found was three inches taller than before – along with the rest of him.

"Alastair," he said, "do you stay close to me."

I looked at him. Was his hair longer, wilder – or was it merely tangling in the wind? Were his shoulders broader, his chest wider? I had no more chance to look upon him than he was off again and driving hard with wooden staff to speed his way. Staff?! My head began to swim a little, as if a dram or two of malt had, of a sudden, filled my blood. I understood but little – apart from this one thing that grew upon me as I struggled to keep pace and the rain began in earnest and drove against us: I feared for something, I knew not what, and this man was what stood between myself and it.

Jamie did not stop – haste was his concern – but he pointed towards the loch with his staff as he walked. I would hazard it was still a mile distant; the light was subdued to a dull, dismal greyness and I strained to see through shards of rain, but when I raised my hood I could just make it out across the water, a white stone building, larger than a cottage. It was madness, but for reasons I did not understand, I knew this was sanctuary and I realised then that I had been fighting to keep a fluttering alarm deep to the pit of my stomach, in order for it not to rise and turn to something worse. It was mad, unreasoned, but I felt relief at the sight of that structure.

"Aye, there, there she is! Come, Alastair, come!"

He strode forward at a rush, and I followed as closely as I could. Thunder broke above the hills and rolled swiftly down the glen; it crashed again and lightning fizzed a jagged path from sky to earth. Again, again...the wind twisted and rushed and howled, yet I heard a voice rise above it, and recall it still.

"So, ye Campbells!!" it roared, "ye think to make your homestead?!"

Two men stood in our path. A third smiled grimly as he balanced, sure-footed, on a boulder, legs akimbo; it was he who had cried out amongst the maelstrom and, from his manner, I feared there was as much violence within him as the storm.

Let me describe him.

First, his size. Upon his boulder he had loomed large but even when he stepped down from it, to my eyes he still looked to be a giant of a man, taller even than my companion, who had somehow grown to be two or three inches above the six feet; if I felt insignificant – and I did – beside these wild men it was not to be surprised at.

And wild they were. The man himself, the leader as his manner declared, was clothed in the great kilt or plaid of double tartan, laid in folds around him up to and above his chest and underlaid with a tunic of saffron. The rain had soaked these through but he was not a man to notice such trifles; indeed, his thighs were bare and the muscles brawny and he wore only short buskins to the calf to protect his legs in the vilest of weathers. It was above the neck that I caught the measure of the man. His forehead was broad, hair plastered upon it, and his face could have been of the granite upon which he had been standing – stony and hard. Perhaps the only emotion that could express upon it was that of hatred – as it did now. If I had doubts about this I had only to look at his eyes, which were deep set and blazed blue-black. The smile I discarded as being one without joy – perhaps it was merely grim satisfaction at having three men against two and that of having a Campbell within his grasp.

For I had recognised the tartan. Aye, the Clan MacDonald! At which, history was alive before me – it surrounded me; I became one with it. The ancient feud, the massacres, the blood spilled...and Glencoe...not to be forgiven or forgotten.

I looked at Jamie and saw that he was full dressed now in winter Highland clothes of a kind with the men before him – but the colouring of his tartan was blue and black as against the green of the MacDonalds. These attires were not of woven cloth cut fashionable to these times; they were of bygone days – as were the weapons they wielded.

"Stay ye behind me, Archie, and when the chance arises, run! Run for the homestead and the kinfolk, run as though your life depends upon it – for it does!"

The name – it was not mine! But I had not time to ponder this.

I carry the picture in my mind to this day. His right hand gripped a broadsword and his left a dirk, and the two men who could contain themselves no longer roared and rushed at him, one to each side. The weapons they brandished were similar to his own and when they neared he whirled the sword above and around his head. The wind whistled and whooped across the blade as he slashed down to left and right and the clash of steel rang through me, and I did as he had bid; I ran, though the fibre of my being wished to stay and help – but what was I? A man out of his time? No, it was more: I was a boy amongst men! So, yes, I did what I was told.

I wish...I wish that I had been stronger, swifter, surer – perhaps I would have reached that sanctuary; perhaps Jamie, the Spectre of Dearg, would no longer be compelled to traverse that windswept glen as protector along the stormy corridors of time.

But the fury that was MacDonald was before me, barring my way, claymore in hand, and no matter which way I turned, blinded by the rain, he would not let me pass. He raised his blade.

"Get ye back, Archie!" And I felt a strong arm, no spirit at that moment but flesh and blood and muscle and bone, push me aside. "To Rutthers then!"

I turned and ran. I slipped and slid alongside the stream, which now rushed with the force of torrential falling water, and passed two bodies along the way; Jamie had cut them down and they lay, bloody and still, wild no longer.

I halted once only on that flight along the glen. The rain beat against me and my lungs heaved fit to burst – but terror has a way of brushing such bodily concerns aside and so I looked back only when I had reached the foot of the hill path towards Rutthers. The rain had eased a little but darkness would be upon me within the hour, therefore I strained to see who it was that stared across bleak, saturated heather and gorse, blackening in the failing light. A man lay at his feet – whether Campbell or MacDonald, I could not say.

And so, those of you who have stayed with me – the listeners, the curious and the enlightened – I would explain the matter as best I can. For, when at witching hour I knocked them up at Frasier's Farm, irritable at first then alarmed, as could be told by widened eyes, and I stumbled unkempt and wild across the door, the landlady sat me down and bid her daughter bring me spirit. Then she told me what she knew.

1698. The brothers Campbell, as close as brethren could ever be, being waylaid by Gregor MacDonald and two companions in the Glen Dearg, were beaten back by blade and number, such that the elder, Jamie, called for Archie to run for home around the loch. He would not at first, until Jamie cried out with passion that he would hold and fight until he returned with kin, and so he did; yet Gregor cruelly cut him down as he passed.

Then it was that these great scions fought – Campbell and MacDonald – whilst three bodies lay nearby. It was said of them, the landlady told, that a bloodier fight between a pair could not be imagined, for the cuts upon Campbell before he succumbed were many and he died where he fought, whilst the MacDonald himself lived but briefly after.

"Ah, I have it now," I said to mother and daughter. "Jamie cannot rest until Archie – or some lone stranger who takes his place – makes refuge as he had bid."

They nodded in return and the daughter laid a blanket over my knees. The fire, which they had kindly stoked, and the whisky freely given and imbibed moved me towards sleep, yet it was not welcome. For I feared this: that I might dream of those poor souls combatting for eternity, clamouring and clanging and never truly dying in the bloody Glen Dearg.

WHEN WILL I SEE YOU AGAIN?
By Tony Ormerod

My dear Sir Francis,

I write this in a considerable temper – and you know very well what that could mean for your future well-being.

One never knows where one is with you these days; nor indeed where you are. I write more in hope than anticipation that you will receive this. Have I not, on more than one occasion, made it clear to you that my permission to carry out raids on Spain and her colonies is given only on condition that I receive the lion's share of the "booty", as you call it?

The Spanish ambassador has just left my presence after much wailing and gnashing of teeth for well over an hour. I could hardly get a word in – which, as you know, is most unusual and, even allowing for his exaggerations, I concede that he has a point.

'How would you like it, your Majesty,' he enquired, 'if some of our brave Spanish lads sailed into Dover, or Portsmouth, or Birmingham and proceeded to pillage, plunder and burn unchecked?'

I stopped myself from pointing out that the last location was landlocked but permitted myself a slight smile at his poor grasp of geography. But that is neither here nor there. We are not amused. I very much doubt if I can go on making excuses for your conduct unless, of course, you come up with most of the proceeds of your adventures, in which case I shall turn a blind eye – but prithee do not continue to try my patience.

Your good friend, but not mine, Sir Walter Raleigh, pushed his luck once too far too often with me. His rather lame attempt to drown me in a large puddle by laying out his cloak on the flimsy pretext that it would somehow shield me from harm was the last straw. A pointless gift of a sack of muddy hard objects (I think he called them potatoes) had already upset me a couple of years before. What is one supposed to do with them – eat them? That, coupled with an unwanted brown weed-like substance that

I had to spit out lest it should poison me, had already indicated that he is an enemy of the state. For these treasonable offences, together with his marrying without my consent, he languishes in the Tower, preparing to meet the executioner.

Is it your wish to share his fate? Do not presume on my good nature by delaying any longer from dropping anchor in England at the earliest opportunity if you knoweth what is good for you.

Elizabeth R

P.S. I hear that you have taken up the latest fashionable game – bowls. I am considered to be something of an expert in these parts and I refute the suggestion that everyone lets me win through fear of the axe. Perhaps we could arrange a game, should you decide to grace us with your presence? Heads says I will win.

DANCEHALL DREAMS
By Jan Brown

"I'm worried about Mum; she's getting quieter and quieter these days." Sarah caressed her mug, even though it was empty of tea.

"Yes, she does seem very withdrawn." Peter nodded in her general direction. "Look, gone off to sleep again."

Because you two can be so bloody boring. Maureen kept her eyes closed and concentrated on looking asleep.

"Do you think we should arrange for a carer to 'live-in', or even think about a nursing home?" Peter asked his older, presumably wiser, sister.

"Don't you dare." Maureen's once sparkling eyes, now a murky shade of seaweed, snapped open.

"Oh-ho, so you were awake! Mum's playing a little game with us." Sarah winked overtly at her brother.

"For goodness' sake, Sarah, don't do that winking thing. Your mouth gapes open and you look really foolish."

"Come on, Mum, we're just concerned about you, sitting here on your own for hours. Wouldn't it be nice to have some company?"

"I'm not completely helpless; believe it or not, I can find my own company if I want any. Now go away, the pair of you, and stop disturbing me. And don't creep out looking all hurt and offended, that'll bring round Mrs Hooper from number 64 and I'll never get rid of her," Maureen cautioned her departing children. Then she added, more gently, "I know you care."

In the blessed silence, Maureen thought about her beloved Ron.

You're gorgeous, you are. He had told Maureen she was gorgeous every day, from their first meeting at the railway station. *Can I hold your hand?* He had tried that every day too since they first met, but even after carefully orchestrated meetings turned into officially walking out together Maureen knew what happened to girls who were too eager to give their heart away.

You'll wait until I'm ready, Ron Spencer. If you think I'm worth waiting for, of course. She'd daringly tweaked the stray curl at the nape of his neck and dodged away, laughing gleefully.

Maureen shifted awkwardly in her bed as her recent hip replacement began to throb again. "I do try to exercise it," she'd assured the doctor, "but it hurts. I'm not some young floozy from Strictly Come Dancing, you know, jumping about."

"No one is suggesting that, Mrs Spencer, but you must keep mobile. In fact, a turn around the dance floor wouldn't hurt you at all." He'd nodded encouragingly at her, his golf-ball eyes magnified behind the huge glasses. "Will you try for me? Join a class, maybe?"

She'd bowed her head and pretended to sleep until she knew he was gone.

It was so easy to believe they were together again, holding hands and dancing to the big band sound in the Rivoli Ballroom. The harsh remaining memories of the Second World War diminished by the luxury of plush red velvet seating, almost a forbidden treat. The glittering centrepiece chandelier – far more beautiful than anything the BBC props department could create – twinkling in the seductive evening shadows. Maureen and Ron holding hands, floating blissfully around the polished floor to Sinatra's Moon River *or emotions overflowing at the desperate entreaties of Engelbert's* Last Waltz.

"I miss you, Ron," Maureen whispered, eyes clamped shut to prevent the tears falling. Caught in a sleepy netherworld of dream and reality, she could almost smell the Paco Rabanne he had favoured, enthusiastically dousing himself in the scent. Maureen smiled as she recalled accusing him of 'trying to attract other women'. She sniffed again. That smell.

"I only ever had eyes for you, Maureen. You know that, don't you?"

"I miss you so much, Ron." She spoke into the empty room. "I want to be with you now."

"It's not right for you, not yet. Peter and Sarah still need you."

"But what about me, what I want?"

"Listen, my girl, my heart was worn out. I had to go, but you've got some more dancing in you yet." A sob rose from

Maureen's throat but was magically stilled as she felt tender pressure on her shoulders. *"Just promise me you'll be dancing with me in your heart, never mind what bloke's holding your hand."*

Maureen became aware of a bell ringing incessantly, followed by what she realised was the front door knocker banging relentlessly.

"Hello? I say, it's Connie Hooper from number 64. Are you ok in there?"

Unwillingly, Maureen heaved herself off the bed. *Oh Ron, she never gives me a minute's peace, that woman.* She began the slow laborious shuffle on her bum down the stairs.

What do you think, my darling Ron? Perhaps I should see if she wants to go to a tea dance one Sunday. Until you and I meet again, of course.

ABOUT THE AUTHORS

The TEN GREEN JOTTERS of Sidcup:

Jan Brown

Jan Brown, aka Emily the Writer, has always loved writing, ambitiously penning her own Starsky & Hutch story at the age of 12, although she never actually allowed anyone else to read it.

Jan has had a number of articles, interviews and short stories published and is a prize winner in, and regular contributor to, The Monthly Seagull magazine and to the Charlton Athletic fanzine. She lives with her husband, Richie Snashall (reader, I married him) and still loves anything furry with four legs.

Glynne Covell

Married, with two children, and grandchildren, her hobbies of travelling, history and calligraphy all have links with her writing for which she has a very special passion (this, and chocolate!). She is delighted to be able to contribute to this, the third anthology by the Ten Green Jotters of Sidcup.

Julia Gale

Originally from Carlisle, then brought up in Southampton, Julia moved to London in 1995 after marrying her husband, Colin. Julia was a prodigious early reader as a child. Always with a book in her hand this may well have fuelled her desire to become an author, and she began by writing poems for the local church magazine. Over the years she has had a variety of jobs but since being married has been a full-time mother and house wife, occasionally finding time to do voluntary work; with Colin, she has three grown up daughters and a disabled son. Her hobbies are cooking and gardening.

Her observations on people, the real-life situations they find themselves in and life's many ups and downs are reflected in her stories.

C.G Harris

C. G Harris hails from Kent, England, UK. He is a former winner of the *William Van Wert Award* for a fiction short story. His book *Light and Dark: 21 Short Stories* was shortlisted for the *"Words for the Wounded" Independent Author Award*. His second collection, *Kisses from the Sun and Other Stories* was released in June 2020. His third book features the 1940s Manhattan detective Aaron Baum.

He has a wife, two daughters, four grandchildren, one dog and a cat. He plays the guitar, ukulele and juggles...although not necessarily all at the same time.

A.J.R. Kinchington

Edinburgh born she currently lives in London.

A writing competition win at eleven years old started her on a life-long love of story-telling. Three children and a twenty-five-year career in psychotherapy gave little time to write for pleasure but a note book to jot down ideas was always to hand. Travel to many countries has been an inspiration and now retired she has time for the necessity to write.

Joining the Ten Green Jotters has given her the encouragement to continue to put pen to paper.

Richard Miller

Richard has lived most of his life in Sidcup, birthplace of the Ten Green Jotters. Although much of his working career was spent in London as a Network and Telecommunications

Manager in a Government Department, his job also required him to visit more exotic locations including Barbados. India, South Africa and Thailand.

He is a season ticket holder at Chelsea and enjoys real ale, whisky, blues music and history. At home Richard has several hundred books and records plus several bottles of single malt whisky. He is a member of a number of historical societies and is on the committee of one of them. Richard is researching his family history and has traced one branch back to the 17th Century.

Tony Ormerod

Derby born, and dreaming of journalism, at 16 Tony inexplicably rejected a job offer with the local *Evening Telegraph*. Employment in the warm bosom of Local Government beckoned and then, migrating way down South [Hove], he progressed to Bromley Council where he was later declared surplus to requirements. A career in financial services led to early retirement and an ambition to do nothing was achieved.

Occasionally, this idleness is interrupted by articles published in the aforementioned newspaper plus a couple more in the 'Best of British' magazine. After 54 years he remains married to the same lovely wife. She pleads anonymity.

Richie Stress

Richie has always liked words. He has used them to write short stories, scripts for television and award-winning poetry. In 2008 he was talked into studying for a Creative Writing degree by a very enthusiastic lady from the Open University...and which he completed a mere seven years later. He lives in Orpington with his new wife and his favourite animal is the snow leopard.

Janet Winson

Janet hopes that you enjoy her three stories within this collection; they all have their roots in family life and past events - with some poetic license!

Reading has been a big part of her life from earliest days, plus a love of cinema and theatre that has continued and grown during retirement. The writing bug came later and she was greatly inspired after taking a Creative Writing course during which she met other like-minded individuals and they went on to form the Ten Green Jotters writing group. Meeting monthly, Janet and the rest of the group share literary creation and friendship. She hopes you enjoy this third collection of stories from the group.

Lily the Dog

Lily is the honorary member and mascot of the group. She is eight years old, a springer spaniel, and her interests consist of eating, "squirrel-chasing" by day and "fox-watching" in the evening. She was inspired to join the group after reading that Timmy the dog was a founder member of the Famous Five. She has not displayed any literary talent as yet but the remainder of the group remain optimistic

Printed in Poland
by Amazon Fulfillment
Poland Sp. z o.o., Wrocław

27174144R00077